T0381954

THE REST OF OUR LIVES

Praise for *The Rest of Our Lives*:

'Pitch perfect in its first-hand delivery, its faithful depiction of the small failings and misfortunes of a life, *The Rest of Our Lives* resonates gloriously and sometimes momentously with our own.' Jane Feaver

'A compelling journey across America, and deep inside one man's troubled psyche. Engrossing, moving and original.' Ian Rickson

BEN MARKOVITS

The Rest of Our Lives

faber

First published in 2025
by Faber & Faber Ltd
The Bindery, 51 Hatton Garden
London ECIN 8HN

Typeset by Faber & Faber Ltd
Printed in the UK by CPI Group (UK) Ltd, Croydon, CRO 4YY

A CIP record for this book
is available from the British Library

ISBN 978-0-571-38854-7

2 4 6 8 10 9 7 5 3

To Caroline

I

When our son was twelve years old, my wife had an affair with a guy called Zach Zirsky, whom she knew from synagogue. He was a little younger, three or four years, had three boys, all younger than our two kids, but was in some sense in the same position as my wife—they both had partners who made good money, which meant they didn't have to do much and got bored and restless and maybe even depressed. Zach's wife was head of oncology at Westchester County. I saw Zach touch Amy's hand under the foldout table at the Purim food bank drive, under the paper cloth. He was short, about five-eight, broad-shouldered and dark. He wore linen shirts open at the chest; his chest hair had started going gray. On Sundays, he played guitar for the kids at Temple Beth and taught them Jewish songs, like "Spin Spin Sevivon"—very pro-Israel, in a tree-planting, happy-clappy way. He was the kind of guy who danced with all the old ladies and little pigtailed girls at a bar mitzvah, so he could also put his arm around the pretty mothers and nobody would complain. Even before I saw them holding hands I didn't like him.

My parents are Catholic but my dad thought religion was just a big fancy dress party, and he hated fancy dress. Maybe this is why I never got involved in the synagogue, which meant Amy had a whole social network where she had an identity and I didn't.

She told me about Zach after I already knew and after it was already over. Amy had highly developed guilt feelings, which were so strong she couldn't help being mad at whoever she felt guilty toward. Which was often me. She said she wanted to make me mad, too; she just wanted some kind of reaction, that's all she was looking for, but that's not really my style. If there's something you can do to fix something, I try to do it. But in this case, I wasn't sure what. She said, you don't feel anything about anything. I said, everything I do I do for you and the kids. Nothing else matters to me.

So what do you want to do? I asked her. Do you want a divorce?

But she didn't want that. At least, not until the kids had left home—the home and the kids were all she had to show for the last twelve years of her life. The thing with Zach didn't mean anything. It was more like a kind of self-harm. (She knew that I knew that when she was a teenager she used to cut herself on the thigh.) A bid for attention. But Amy's a person who tells stories about her motives and actions, which are very persuasive, to her as well, so it's sometimes hard to talk about or even work out what's really going on.

You fall in love with somebody when you're twenty-six, and you see them in all kinds of different lights and according to their potential, but after years and years of marriage and shared parenting and all the other shared decisions you have to make just to get through the days, you accumulate a lot of data about that person that after a while just seems . . . more or less accurate. If you continue to have illusions, that's your fault. So if you stay married it's because you've accepted that this is what they're like, and what your life with them is like, and you stop expecting them to do or give you things you know perfectly well they're unlikely to do or give you. It's like being a Knicks fan.

But I also made a deal with myself. When Miriam goes to college, you can leave, too. Maybe this was just another one of those illusions, but it helped me get through the first few months after Amy told me about Zach, and for the sake of the kids we had to pretend that everything was fine. When in fact what we obviously had, even when things smoothed over, was a C-minus marriage, which makes it pretty hard to score much higher than a B overall on the rest of your life.

Twelve years later, Miriam turned eighteen. We spent the first few weeks of August on Cape Cod. Amy's family had a house in Wellfleet, which you had to book a year in advance; and even then there was a lot of overlapping and arguing about beds. It had a studio in the yard where you could potentially sleep as many people as you had mattresses for, and for that reason, in one corner there was a pile of old mattresses under the eaves. If you didn't mind sharing a bathroom or walking out in the morning to take a leak off the deck. Normally I stayed in the city and came up only on the weekends, but it was Miriam's last summer at home, so I took two weeks off.

Amy's big brother Richard had the main house with his new wife—they had a new baby. His other two kids were in their thirties, one of them had a baby of her own. That's why they got the house and we got the studio, which seemed reasonable to me, although Amy thought it was just another example of how her family prioritized Richard. Her dad, whom she idolized, had died years ago, when Amy was still in high school. Her relationship with her mother was more complicated. Anyway, one of the funny little things that happened is that Esther (Amy's mother) let Richard and Kelsey stay in the master bedroom, which had the only *en suite*, even though in the past when we shared the house with Esther, she insisted on sleeping in her own room. That's because Tom only came for the weekend, she explained. (I'm Tom.)

So on some level of course it was my fault.

But there are too many Naftalis to keep track of them all, and most of them don't matter to this story.

I met Amy in grad school in Boston. She was doing her Master's in Education, while I was in my third year of a PhD on the sixties American novel—just at the point where you have to start writing, so I fantasized about dropping out and going to law school. Amy was actually dating a friend of mine, Ethan Konchar, until he won a fellowship to the Max Planck Institute in Göttingen. The farewell party was at his apartment in Somerville, which he shared with another grad-school buddy, Sam Tierney.

Amy was an unusually beautiful woman but also nice about it. Her strategy was just to like, keep still, so she didn't give off false flares; but naturally it meant she also drew a lot of attention. People at the party kept commiserating with her, because Ethan was going away, and she's the kind of person who wants to please people by acting and feeling what they expect her to feel. That night she got stuck in the kitchen, where the drinks were, and people came up to her and said things like, When are you going to see him again? At that point it still wasn't clear if they were staying together. She's about five-ten, with terrific posture—for most of her childhood she wanted to be a ballerina, but then got too big. Amy doesn't actually look particularly Jewish. She has long brown curly hair, which she wears past her shoulders, and a strong handsome Waspy face. She even modeled for a wrist-watch company in college; she looks like the kind of woman who can ride a horse, which she actually can. For her last two years of high school she went to Brearley, after her dad died and they moved back to New York.

I got her number from Ethan and called a few weeks after the party to see how she was doing. He said they'd split up, but even when we started dating she felt like she was cheating on him, which made the first few months much more intense than with anybody else I ever went out with. It was a big deal for her, when she invited me to the Cape before Christmas.

In those days I still felt like the older guy—I was twenty-six, she was twenty-three. I had a car, a Toyota Corolla I bought by working as a customer service agent for Alaska

Airlines. I used to spend weekends out at Logan: from curb to cabin, that was my responsibility. We drove out on Route 6, while the continent narrowed around us, and even though it was about twenty degrees outside (but bright, icy winter sunshine), she made me stop at the Wellfleet Dairy Bar and Mini-Golf. Though of course it was closed, out of season; she just wanted to show me. Every summer before they went up to the house, her dad pulled over to buy them ice creams. This was my first real contact with the little childish rituals rich people have toward some of the blessings in their lives.

So when we got to the house, before unpacking, we had to walk down to the beach. You reached it from a steep wooden staircase, then stumbled across the marram grass to the water. Like I said, it was twenty degrees, about three in the afternoon. This was on the Bay side, though I didn't really understand the geography. There was a little old snow on the dunes, but not much wind—the sea looked like a sea.

Amy was very very happy to be there. In schoolgirl mode, but very very happy. The house itself, when I was finally allowed to look around, turned out to be totally charming. The Naftalis first moved there in the thirties. Amy's grandfather knew Hayden Walling, who built a lot of the houses in Wellfleet, and extended theirs, which started out as a traditional Cape Cod. Walling added a wing and a second floor. None of it matched, but everything blended together. You know the kind of thing, old rugs, Shaker furniture . . . I didn't at the time. I thought, this is the kind of life I want to inherit.

6

The basic style was utilitarian chic. In the kitchen, instead of using cupboards, pots and pans hung from hooks on the wall. The sink was under the window, with a view of the Bay. Boards creaked underfoot. There weren't any curtains downstairs, so you got big slabs of light lying at odd angles over the floor and leaning on the walls, from the low sun. But there was also a lot of accumulated family history, including a strange little birdman painting by Max Ernst. Amy pointed it out. "The one thing that's actually worth something," she said. "Dad met him." On the wall over the dining-room table hung a row of head shots, of Amy's grandfather and his three brothers—black-and-white studio portraits. All of them turned out to be highly successful people in different fields. Two of them made real money.

But there were also things like ... one of Amy's kindergarten pictures, glued bits of sea glass, and real sand and grass, and the sea painted in Crayola green. Framed and hung up at the foot of the stairs.

Amy was a late sleeper, until we had kids. I got up early to work but really just wandered around. The house had no central heating—they used rusty old gas-canister heaters, which had wheels and that you had to light with a match. I didn't trust myself so made coffee and warmed my hands on that. Some of the sofas and chairs had wool blankets draped over them. The big wall of glass in the living room faced west, so in the morning it was all in shade.

We stayed a week, before her brother came with his first wife. But there was no overlap. It snowed heavily halfway

7

through and the roads only just cleared in time for us to drive back to Boston, where I dropped her off at her apartment and then drove on to Trenton, where my mother lived. On her own, so I always spent Christmas with her. Over the break I started studying for my LSATs and formally dropped out of grad school a few months later. By that point I was already in love with Amy and figured that for the kind of life we might want to have together I needed to make more money. But I didn't want to write the book anyway.

Miri's boyfriend came up for the weekend. His arrival provoked a lot of family discussion, I mean, among the Naftalis generally. For most of the year, they never called or wrote each other, but still, whenever they got together they had this sense of a shared culture or tradition to uphold, which made them seem closer than they were. Part of it was an old-fashioned prudish streak, which Amy had too, even though she sometimes rebelled against it.

In the end, Jim brought a tent and set it up in the yard, and we let Miri sneak out to join him even though officially she was still sleeping in the studio with us.

The weekend was not a total success. Jim was going to Harvard—he'd spent the summer interning at Apple Park, which meant that Miri basically thought of them as broken-up. She was happy to see him again to say goodbye but wanted to start her own college life (at Carnegie Mellon) with a clear deck. Anyway, he told a lot of stories about Cupertino. Everybody you met was relaxed but also incredibly smart and hardworking. That kind of thing, which annoyed Miri, though maybe there were other tensions going on; they bickered a lot. Amy hated this kind of public display, especially in front of her brother.

"Miriam," she said, in her let's-be-a-good-girl voice. "Play nicely."

Once, she even apologized to Jim. "I'm sorry, Jim," she said. "She gets it from her father. No, let me explain," because she realized how that came across. "I mean, the Laywards don't think you have to be polite to people you care about. Isn't that true? That's what you always say to me."

"That's true," I said. And she was right, I didn't mind.

Jim was actually a nice kid. He was only about five-eight but clean-cut and good-looking, and one of five finalists for Westchester/Putnam High School Wrestler of the Year. He didn't win and took it all with good grace. (There was some kind of poll on social media, sponsored by the local paper, in which he came fourth.) It didn't matter, you could tell where he was headed: Harvard, then San Francisco or Wall Street . . . by the end of his twenties he'd be making seven figures. I liked him, but I also thought, in high school there's no way I'm friends with this kid. He always had a respectful attitude toward me, but I don't think he saw law professor as his first-choice career.

One afternoon, there was a big family party at the Brinkmans', old friends of Amy's parents who had a house overlooking Slough Pond. This party was an end-of-summer tradition. People brought potluck, and there was a twenty-foot wooden table in the yard, with benches on either side, where everybody sat down to eat. The water was close enough you could almost jump in from the decking. Kids ran around, there was a dock and a boathouse, and Miri and Jim took some of the grandchildren out in a couple of canoes. Anyway, Jim started horsing around—he wanted Amy to race him, but then he pulled too hard and the canoe tipped over. The little Brinkman in his boat was only nine years old, but the water wasn't cold and the kid could swim.

It wasn't a big deal. They were only twenty feet from the shore, but for some reason Miri got upset with him, and they had a fight on the beach in front of everybody.

Amy said, "Tom, you have to step in."

"Why me?"

"Because she resents me whenever I try to tell her anything." Which was true.

"What do you want me to do?"

"I don't know, but this can't go on anymore."

That kind of language always gets my back up, but I stood up anyway. "Hey, Miri. Hey, Jim," I said, walking down the rotten wooden stairs. "Let's keep it down a little, hey."

"Butt out," Miri said.

"I'm sorry, Mr. Layward. It was my fault—I used too much torque."

"You were showing off."

"Walk with me," I said to Miri.

"I told you to butt out," but in the end she came along, and Jim went back to the house to get changed.

"Did Mom send you?" she asked.

"What does it matter?"

"She only cares about what it looks like."

"It looks like you guys aren't having much fun."

There isn't any path along the water, but you can walk into the trees and through the trees back up to the road, which is a very pretty road, with a few houses on it, mostly hidden by trees.

My daughter (I'm fairly convinced) is going to be a competent, reasonable adult, but at this stage she was caught up in her own concerns, which made her seem more selfish than she is. "He always has to win at everything," she said. "Even if it's not a competition, for him, it's a competition. Which is fine, it's what he's like. But he thinks he can like, win me. Like, if we disagree about something, he just has to be more persuasive. I'm sorry," she said. "I've probably told you this before."

"That's fine. People repeat themselves when they're trying to work something out."

But that was the wrong thing to say. "That's not at all what's going on. I told him, I love you, but you don't want me hanging around your neck when you get to Harvard."

"What'd he say to that?"

"I don't know."

"What'd he say?"

"I don't know, Dad. Something like, that's not how I think about it, or it doesn't have to be like that . . . I don't want to talk about it anymore."

It was about eighty degrees, just perfect coastal summer weather, the kind only rich people can afford. In the shade of the trees you almost felt chilly, but then you walked into a patch of sun. One of the things in life that I'm grateful for is that my daughter believes I totally adore her; that even when she screws up or gets something wrong, she has no real faults; that she has nothing to prove with me, which is not how she feels around her mother. But maybe this is what fathers always tell themselves. Amy says to me, "You think she opens up with you, but she doesn't; she just tells you what she knows you want to hear."

What do I want to hear? Not the stuff she tells me, but Amy thinks I have no idea what girls are like. The way they design their personalities to please other people, which is what she says she did. But Miri doesn't actually care that much about other people; she's more like me.

"There's another way of looking at this," I said to her. "Which is, that he's not very good at paddling and fell in the water."

"We have to fight about something. Otherwise it'll be too hard on Monday."

Monday he was driving back to New York so he could pack for Harvard.

"You don't have to break up with him. People stick it out."

"I'm not worried it's the wrong decision or anything. I just have to make it through the next few days."

Even before we returned to the Brinkmans', she started texting Jim. Or texting somebody—that part of the Cape has very poor reception, so whenever we went anywhere with a signal, Miri pulled out her phone. I figured we had talked enough anyway; you could hear party sounds drifting through the trees. It was about four in the afternoon and just windy enough for the sun to dazzle a little when it hit the water. Apart from the phone, we might have been in any decade of the last fifty years. Sometimes around seaside resorts I get this half-remembered sense of myself as a young man who doesn't know what's going to happen with the rest of his life and doesn't much care.

Lunch had been cleared away when we got back. At some point, Leslie Brinkman brought out two large apple strudels, which she had made herself, and cut them up on the long table. There were paper plates and a bowl of sour cream so people could help themselves. Then it was five o'clock, and Danny Brinkman, who was in his seventies, decided to make cocktails. His son carried the bar cart from the living room onto the deck, so he could wheel it around . . . sea breezes, old-fashioneds, he even put on an apron. What can I get you, sir? He had large, dry, arthritic hands that trembled when he tried to pick up ice from the bucket with rubber tongs.

I figured I might as well get drunk. Aside from other reasons, so Amy would have to stay sober enough to drive. These are the games you play. At parties we're always quietly aware of each other but don't interact much. Sometimes I see her talking to strangers, or people I don't know, and she's so . . . hemmed in by her . . . poise that she has nothing new or interesting to say. Even though she is still the most handsome woman at the party, people find excuses to get away from her, which is maybe why she started drinking more, although she usually regrets it afterward.

The first time Zach Zirsky talked to her, at someone's bar mitzvah, or the first time I noticed them talking, I remember being pleased for Amy, because it gave her a buzz to be flirted with. He has a manner that people sometimes get praised for, of treating you like you're the only person in the room, which always seems creepy to me. But fine, what do I care. It's nice for her to get a little attention.

Later, I asked her how it started. Who made the first move. She said, I invited him to lunch. Zach was a freelance filmmaker, which can mean almost anything. Amy, after she gave up teaching, had a lot of ideas about educational documentaries, where you basically have a captive audience, which is why the standard is often so low. So he offered to talk her through these ideas. He said he could put her in touch with a few people. Have you ever done any acting? Oh, no, I can't be on camera, I'm much too self-conscious, etc. This is how I imagine their conversations. Amy said, he was always very supportive of me. He was very supportive of your adultery, I said. Don't turn it all into something like that. Even after it was over . . . he thought I had something to offer, that I wasn't getting the chance . . . to use *all* of myself . . .

But she knows I hate it when people talk like that.

It used to be when I drank I talked more, now I talk less. Miri had one of the babies in her arms, I couldn't tell them apart, maybe Uncle Richard's kid. She was trying to get him to sleep, which was also a strategy for preoccupying herself so Jim had to leave her alone. At a certain stage, if you're not talking, and are feeling generally out of the picture, you become sensitive to things like that. I felt sad for my kid, who had to learn to protect herself because Jim was going away. Of course, she was going away too, and I hadn't protected myself against that.

Later, I found myself in a group with Danny Brinkman and his son Jeffrey, who teaches economics at Rindge and Latin, and my impression is has a pretty nice life. He works as a public high school teacher but lives in a big house off Porter Square and spends his summers in places like this. Anyway, he was telling stories about one of his students, who was sometimes a she and sometimes a he, and Jeffrey couldn't work out if this was supposed to be apparent to him, because they sometimes wore short skirts to class and sometimes big jeans, big shirt, etc.

"For which we used to have a very good word, which nobody uses anymore," I said.

"Which is what?" Jeffrey asked. "The truth is, I like this kid a lot. They seem free from some of the stupid stuff I had to wrestle with at their age. Part of me is just jealous."

"Transvestite."

"Come on, Dad," Miri said. It was around seven o'clock, and the sun was going down across the water and in my eyes.

"You know they've . . . we're supposed to add a line under our university emails, which says like, he/his/him, which I refuse to do. So I got an email from the compliance officer."

"There's no such thing as a compliance officer," Miri said.

"Anyway, I started signing off with he/I/mine. So I get another email and have to explain myself. I don't like being referred to in the accusative. It literally objectifies I."

"He didn't say this. He didn't do any of these things."

"How do you know?" I said, putting my arm around Miri. "How do you know what I get up to when you're not around?"

But Amy had joined us now—we were heading home.

"What's he getting up to?" she said.

"Nothing, Dad's just talking."

"I never talk when I'm drunk, I become very observant."

"Angry white male," Miri said. This is what she calls me, when she thinks I'm trying to be controversial.

Jim was there, too. He was wearing someone else's clothes, which were too big for him and made him look like a different person. Not like a Harvard guy at all.

"How come you never hear me raise my voice," I said. "If I'm so angry? Explain that—how come I'm always the mildest-mannered guy in the room?"

"Come on, Dad."

"Thank you for the shirt, Mr. Brinkman," Jim said. "I'm sorry about the boat."

"Don't worry about it," Jeffrey said. "These things happen."

It was quiet in the car on the way home—the drive only takes ten minutes. When we got in, Miri went straight to the fridge to see what she could eat. "Didn't you have anything at the party?" Amy said.

"That was like, three hours ago . . ."

"I'm so full I have to lie down."

"Fine, lie down. Does that mean there are literally no plans for dinner?"

Richard was already back, helping to put the baby to bed; so all of these conversations took place while several other things were going on. Vicky, his daughter from the first marriage, who now edited a political blog in D.C., said, "We thought we'd order pizza."

"There is no good pizza around here," Steve said. Steve was married to Lisa, Richard's other daughter. They had a baby to deal with, too; Lisa was giving him a bath. You could hear the water running, even from the kitchen.

"What about JBs?"

"They closed last year. And they weren't good."

"Don't be such a snob . . ."

And so on. Vicky and Steve had their own independent relationship; he worked for the ACLU. They liked to talk politics together.

Eventually Amy said, "Well, I'm so full from all that strudel, I don't think I can eat anything else."

"We can go to CShore, but that means somebody has to drive."

"I can drive," I said, but Miri told me, "You're drunk."

In the end, they ordered Papa Gino's and sat around the dining table playing Bullshit, just the four of them—Jim and Miri and Steve and Vicky. Amy lay down and I went for a walk around the block, with a beer. Sometimes just your presence as a slightly sadder older guy changes the dynamic. But it was nice to see Miri sitting around with her cousins. By the time I came back, Lisa was downstairs too, eating cold pizza; Miri and Jim seemed to be getting along. I left them to it.

Later, back in the studio, when Miri came in to get her stuff before sneaking out to the tent, Amy said to her, "Do you know about the freshman fifteen?"

"What do you mean, do I know?"

"It's just something you have to watch out for, that's all. You're not biologically a child anymore, where it doesn't matter what you eat because you're still growing."

"Is this supposed to be some kind of coded conversation?"

"I just want to make sure you can look out for yourself," Amy said, "before we let you go."

For some reason she was close to tears.

"Is that your big maternal advice? Don't get fat?"

"That's not what I'm saying at all. Tom, do you want to say something?"

"Everybody else was eating pizza too."

"What do you want me to say?" I said.

"Not Lisa."

"What do you mean, not Lisa? She came down and had three slices."

"Well, she's breastfeeding," Amy said. "I was like that too. You can eat anything and still lose weight."

"Oh my God." Miri stared at me, making a face. "Am I fat?"

"You look good to me," I said.

The truth is, she had put on a few pounds over the summer, but I didn't think it mattered.

After she left, we had the room to ourselves. It was an echoey space, with a wall of dark glass on one side and a high, slanted roof. The overhead lighting was totally inadequate, because it was really designed as an artist's studio, for natural light. All we had, next to the mattresses on the floor, was a standing lamp on a long cord that you had to argue about if you wanted to read in bed. But Amy had turned the light out. She said, "It matters because how you think of yourself matters, especially when you're starting somewhere new. She has to realize, it's up to her now to take care of herself and project the kind of person she wants people to treat her as."

"I'm not sure what that means."

She didn't say anything for a while, I thought she might have fallen asleep.

"You really hate me, don't you," she said.

"Of course not. I just don't always agree with everything you do."

Amy's fights with Miri were nothing new. Even when she was little they used to go at it. It's funny, because when Michael was born, Amy felt disappointed—she'd wanted a girl. But she never had trouble with Michael, he was her little helper. So then Miri came along, and Amy had some-one to buy dresses for, and take to ballet class, all of that stuff, except that from the beginning their relationship was one long argument.

Ballet was one of the battle grounds. I actually had to take her, because Miri wouldn't go if Amy drove her. She hated the tutu, she hated the shoes; I had to get her dressed secretly, out of Mommy's sight. Which of course was partly a rebellion but also an excuse to suddenly appear in front of her mother and receive love and applause. Still, she wanted me to drive her because afterward I never said anything about the class, whereas Amy used to criticize.

The thing about ballet is, they try to get you to do things a certain way, they want you to follow instructions. I took the kids to soccer too, which is more like Hobbesian reality, you just have to survive. But ballet is all about copycat precision. Amy's view was, it teaches you how to present yourself properly, which is especially important for girls—boys are given more leeway. My response was, why are we buying into that bullshit, let Miri present herself however she wants. But Amy thought I was kidding myself if I thought this was a fact about the world she could just ignore.

For years I tried to stay out of it, but I couldn't take the skirmishes on Saturday mornings. You work hard all week and then you want a little quiet family time. The dance class met in an old church hall in White Plains, which was near a farmer's market, so I used to drop Miri off and then get myself a coffee and Danish. Then come back for the last five minutes and hold out a piece of focaccia or a salmon bagel, and from a lineup of little girls in first position she'd give me a secret smile.

Even as a kid, she was a little chunky, and Amy tried to get me to cut back on the treats. Anyway, at a certain point, we all gave up; she just stopped going. This was Amy's first disappointment as a mother.

But it wasn't just ballet. Miri liked to try things and then quit. For years she played YMCA soccer, we had a shelf of trophies for her—they used to win county every year. Then she got to high school and refused to try out for the team.

"Nobody I know is trying out," she said.

"What does that matter," I told her. "Once you're on the team you get to know them."

"Now you know what it's like," Amy said to me, almost pleased. "She just doesn't stick at anything." Because sports is what I cared about. But if they don't want to play, you can't make them. You can't make someone have fun. So when I let it slide Amy reproached me for that, too.

"You really don't care about anything, do you. You think people just become successful adults because they . . . feel like it."

This bugged me, especially given that, I didn't go to Brearley, my parents divorced when I was fourteen, my mom worked in a school—not as a teacher, but as one of the secretaries—and I paid my own way through law school, but whatever. You can't say anything in response because anything you say is a much deeper reproach, about their whole personality and career, than you intend. Amy was essentially unemployed. But her view was that the only reason I had an easy relationship with Miri is because I never challenged her on anything, and the only reason I could get away with it is because Amy did all the dirty work. Which was maybe even true, I don't know. But I could never really fight with Miri anyway. She was too much like me.

Her relationship with Jim started at the end of freshman year, and Amy had complicated feelings about that, too. Because even then Jim was clearly a self-disciplined ambitious kid, which Amy hoped might rub off on Miri.

When they started going out, Miri still dressed like . . . Amy's daughter; I mean, she wore the clothes that Amy bought for her. Dresses, skirts. Keds or penny loafers. Jim was the kind of kid who went to church on Sundays with his family, and if he stopped by our house afterward to hang out, he still had on his jacket and tie. But all of that changed for Miri sophomore year. She discovered punk and hip-hop and spent every weekend going into the city with friends. Thrifting, they called it. She'd come home with heavy bags of clothes, most of which she never wore: jeans three sizes too big, shirts with holes in them. Doc Martens, old Nike high-tops.

"I don't even know how she can put on some of these clothes," Amy said to me. "She used to be so finicky."

"Maybe that's a good thing. To have a kid without neuroses." Michael was always an anxious child.

For her sixteenth birthday, Amy wanted to pierce her nose. She'd already had her ears done at thirteen, which I was against, but Amy told me it was none of my business. How is it not my business? You spend your life as a guy getting slammed for objectifying women, and then you have a daughter and you're supposed to stand back and let her spend however long she wants in front of the bathroom mirror, basically turning herself into an object. Well, whatever; if that's the system, it's the system, I don't expect to change the world. But then when Amy wanted me to take a stand about the nose stud, I told her, you already made it clear, this is not my department.

Even though I wasn't thrilled about it either. But Amy was out-of-all-proportion miserable.

"She wants to get back at me for something. I don't understand it."

"She just wants to dress like her friends."

"Which friends? They don't dress like this . . . or at least, not the ones who can look nice if they want to. That's what's so upsetting. She's deliberately trying to make herself ugly. It's like a kind of self-harm."

"I prefer this kind to the alternative," I said, and she gave me a look.

"That's because it's not directed at you."

"If you fight her on this stuff, which you can't control anyway, then pretty soon all of your interactions are fights."

"What do you want to do? Pretend nothing's going on? Just to get along? I'm sorry. Sometimes you have to be an actual parent. You're not her best friend."

Well, Miri got her nose stud, which after a few weeks I didn't even notice. When she had a cold it looked red and uncomfortable, and I felt sorry for her and didn't like feeling sorry, but that's about as much as I felt about it.

Meanwhile, Jim still wore chinos and collared shirts to school. He joined the debate team, which Miri briefly did too, but then she quit senior year, just before they made it to the regional finals in D.C. If they won that, they'd get to go to the World Schools Debating Championships, which was being held in Stuttgart that year, but they didn't win. I don't think Miri minded either way, except for Jim's sake; she doesn't have a regretful personality. She started a band that fall instead, which was called Luggage, and for a few months she spent several hours a day practicing bass guitar. I blew five hundred bucks on a Peavey amp, because I figured there's no point in buying something shitty if she'll just want to upgrade later.

But then a couple of the girls in her band, who had been going out, split up, and that was it. Miri said she was ready for it to end anyway. Even before they broke up they'd been getting on her nerves. She had her college applications to focus on. At least that's what she said to her parents.

I don't want to give the impression that she was a quitter or somebody who didn't know who she was or what she wanted. If anything, the reverse. She was a curious, outgoing teenager who liked to try different things, but was also confident enough to make up her mind about them and decide, okay, I've done that now. People, I mean not just her classmates but her teachers too, saw her as a leader type, because other people tended to get interested in whatever she was interested in. She was somebody whose attention you wanted, maybe because it didn't always last that long.

Also, regardless of how she dressed—in Enyce jeans and Air Jordan 1s . . . she also dyed a pink streak in her hair when she got in to Carnegie Mellon, as a little self-reward (by that point Amy had basically given up, she wasn't our problem for much longer) . . . anyway, whatever she wore, she still looked like a friendly cool camp counselor who you wouldn't mind babysitting your five-year-old girl.

In other words, she was a good kid. We had about one more week of her childhood, then we were all supposed to drive up to Pittsburgh together to drop her off.

But first Jim had to head back to New York.

After breakfast—I mean, the day after the Brinkmans' party—Jim and Miri packed up the tent and loaded up his car, which was a Mazda3 and nicer than what I drove. I could tell Miri was in good-girlfriend mode, folding up the tent poles, pulling hooks out of the grass. Neither one of them talking much. I know my daughter well enough to know that I don't always understand her mood from how she presents herself. So I couldn't tell you if she was miserable or just trying politely to get through an awkward couple of hours. Amy actually turns out to be more on the nose when it comes to this kind of code-breaking, even though she doesn't always know what to do with the information. I mean, how to act.

In this case, she made sandwiches in the kitchen for him to take on the road. From Wellfleet it's about a five-hour drive back to Scarsdale. Miri retreated to the house to help her, which left Jim and me alone in the yard.

Jim said, "I'm sorry about the grass."

There was a square of flattened yellow grass where the tent had stood.

"It doesn't matter, it'll grow back." Then I said, "It's not my grass anyway."

"I don't know if you know what's been . . . under discussion, between Miri and me, about next year. I know she's got a lot going on. We both do. And it feels like we have some big decisions to make, even if we can probably just get through the next few months and see how we feel."

"You don't have to explain yourself to me."

"I just wanted to say, I don't want anything that happens between us to affect how you think about me. I mean," and he laughed, "the Laywards are a big part of my childhood. Your house . . . and I like to think that you're still somebody I can get in touch with. If I need professional advice, or something like that. Like, if I want to apply to law school."

"Of course, Jim. Of course."

"At some point in the future."

"Whenever you want."

Then the "girls" came back out, with a Whole Foods paper bag that looked much too full. Jim shook my hand. And then, after a short hesitation, gave Amy a hug—she was a little taller than him.

"Come on, Tom," Amy said.

"You don't have to leave us alone or anything."

But we left them to it and went back to the main house. Walking up the steps, Amy actually held my hand and then let go to open the front door, which had a screen. Richard and co had gone to Provincetown for the day—it was Lisa's last day, too. Anyway, we had the house to ourselves.

Amy said, "Get away from the window, Tom. Don't watch. What are they doing? They can see you."

"Just talking."

A few minutes later Miri came in. There was a steep gravel drive, and we could hear the Mazda scattering stones as it pulled onto the road.

"I'm fine," Miri said, "but maybe just don't talk to me for about an hour, or until I say so."

"Whatever you want, sweetie." Sometimes, when she was stressed or emotional, Amy calmed herself down by standing in first position, with her heels together. "I just want you to know that whatever you're feeling is totally normal."

"I said, don't talk. I'm having a bath. I haven't slept in like, three days."

To get her clothes, she had to walk out to the studio again; then she came back through the house with her phone in hand. "Are you both just going to stand there for the rest of the day?" she asked and went upstairs. The bathroom was on the second floor; after a minute, you could hear the water running. Amy looked at me.

"What do we do now?" she said.

"Nothing. We don't have to do anything."

Later, in bed, I almost told her what Jim said, about turning to me in the future for professional advice. But I didn't think she'd take it the way I took it, as the kind of thing

27

that explained why Miri was willing to let the relationship run its course. Also, we didn't confide this stuff in each other anymore.

I realize I haven't said much about Michael yet. He was in LA, where he had a summer research fellowship at the Huntington—there was a six-year gap between him and Miri, which obviously shaped their relationship but didn't necessarily make them less close. Maybe it did, I don't know. Michael had become one of those young people who decides that contact with their family is not a source of happiness, so you have to limit it to unavoidable occasions. Obviously, this was directed not at Miri but at Amy and me. He was in middle school when the Zirsky thing happened and more aware than his sister of what was going on. Not that this means he took my side, but he bore more of the brunt.

Since he was in grad school now and made twenty-odd thousand a year and didn't need my money, he could do what he wanted. I don't blame him, but I also find it hard to talk about. For Amy, it was unspeakably painful. Like I said, he was always her little guy. Somehow she blamed me for his gradual detachment, because Michael and I had a slightly competitive relationship, even though what actually started the whole thing . . . but who am I arguing with, and what does it matter. These things happen—families end up a certain way.

Anyway, one of the occasions he thought he couldn't get out of was seeing Miri before she went off to college. At first, we thought he might join us at the Cape, but he decided to fly to New York so he could catch up with some of his high school friends at the same time.

When we drove back from Wellfleet he was already there. He heard the car pull up and came out. I hadn't seen him in eight months, not since Christmas. Even if he didn't like coming home, when he stayed with us he was always the dutiful son and walked outside barefoot to help unload the car.

"Hey," I said, "how ya doing," because the car could wait. Amy and Miri had already given him hugs.

"You don't look well."

This was true. In April I had a mild bout of Covid that lasted the usual ten days, like a chest cold. But six weeks later I started getting other symptoms—palpitations, sudden fatigue; if I went jogging I might have to stop and walk. This had never happened to me before. The symptoms evolved but didn't go away. Three months later I still got a head rush every time I stood up, which driving made worse. Afterward, I had to lean against the roof of the Volvo until the faintness passed. Miri and Amy were used to it. Also to the fact that in the morning I woke up with a swollen face and leaky eyes, which then over the course of the day slowly drained.

"Thanks, nice to see you too." But he just looked at me, so I said, "I told you I was having these issues."

"You need to see a doctor."

"I went to the doctor. He couldn't find anything wrong."

"Something is clearly wrong. You need to deal with it."

29

This is how he talked to me or expressed his love. The truth is, he's a good boy and one reason he hated coming home is that he took on the burden of everything going on. Like Amy, he worries. But it's also true he treated me like somebody who wasn't capable of running his own life anymore, which at the age of fifty-five I resented. Sometimes what I wanted from him was not worry or advice but just a normal father/son interaction.

Earlier in the day, he'd done a big shop at Balducci's. Whenever he flew to New York he rented a car, because he liked to be independent. So as we went in the house he said to his mother, "I filled the fridge," but for dinner he already had plans. He was meeting people in the city.

"Who?" Miri said. When Michael was in high school, Miri was just a cute kid, but as she got older she liked to hang out with his friends, who had known her for years but now saw her in a new light.

So they talked about that for a while; in the end, she went along too. This was part of the point of Michael's coming home, so he could see Miri and give her some last-minute big-brotherly advice. And I liked watching them leave the house together, even if it meant that Amy and I had a taste of things to come, staring at each other across the dining table.

"Can I give you a ride?" I said, but Michael was taking his car. He could park at the station and that way they didn't have to bother me coming home. In three days Miri was going—we had three days left of family life.

Miri had several things to do to get ready for college, a list of stuff to buy, various online courses to work through, on sexual assault and alcohol, on diversity and inclusion . . . A fat information pack came in the mail; we also got a lot of emails from the assistant director of first-year orientation, a guy named Steve Linderman. (His friendly smiling face kept popping up in my Hotmail account.) One of them included contact numbers for Miri's future roommates, so she could call them if she wanted to. This occupied a certain anxious portion of each day. Then her textbooks arrived. She planned to major in Design but had to take a few general education courses too, like Intro Psych and Interpretation and Argument.

"Oh my God, I can't understand any of this."

"Yes you can. Just read it, I mean actually read it, don't just flip through the pages."

We had many conversations like this. A pile of books and papers accumulated at one end of the dining table, which wouldn't be cleared up until we drove Miri to Pittsburgh.

Michael kept trying to push Amy about my medical issues, to take them more seriously. Usually in my presence. "What are we doing about this?" he said. When he came home he liked to sort things out, so he could go away again.

"I don't know that there's anything more we can do. He's talked to Shulquist."

"Shulquist is just a primary care physician. He won't know anything."

"They ran a lot of tests."

"Who did? What tests?" And so on, while I just sat there.

"Your father can look after himself," Amy said at last. "He always does."

Which was true—I didn't expect more from her at this stage of our marriage.

But I liked having Michael to talk to. Sometimes while Amy was making dinner we'd walk to Hyatt Field and shoot hoops for half an hour. It was only a couple of blocks from the house. This is something we used to do when he was a boy, when I got home from work. I really tried to push him into basketball; I played Div 3 in college, it seemed to me one of the things you should pass on to your kids. But I think he just came along to make his father happy.

In August at six o'clock the court was usually empty—if there were kids out late, they played in the playground next door. Michael and I could just shoot around, passing the ball back and forth.

He talked to me about his dissertation (on the limits of a Kantian response to Rawls' theory of justice) and I told him what was going on in my professional life. About six months ago I got a call from Brian Palmetto, one of my old college teammates, who now worked for the Denver Nuggets. Michael had met him; Brian sometimes came out to dinner when he was in New York. Once he got us Knicks tickets, second row seats, and we all went to the Garden together. But this was when Michael was small, maybe seven years old. I remember sitting with Miri strapped to my chest— Amy was worried how she would react, but the noise knocked her out. Anyway, Brian called up because he wanted some legal advice.

A story had come out in *Sports Illustrated* about Terry Kirkland, the Nuggets' majority owner, who over the past two decades had said and done some things that, the story alleged, contributed to a hostile work environment, especially for women and minorities. Even though the Nuggets' track record on hiring both was pretty good. That's one of the things Brian was proudest of. He got along okay with Terry personally, although that's partly, he admitted, because I'm a middle-aged white guy who went to Pomona; I understand he can rub people the wrong way. But the whole thing had been hugely divisive for everybody from the front office on down. Somehow Brian had ended up on the side of ownership, while a lot of the people he liked and respected on the Nuggets had ended up on the other side.

Tough times for me personally, he said, but who cares about me.

Anyway, the league was looking into these allegations and possible sanctions for Kirkland and the franchise. Brian wanted to put me in touch with somebody at the NBA, which had hired the law firm Draxell, Schmidt, Ogilvy and Walters to investigate. One of my areas of expertise is corporate governance—I'd consulted on similar cases for high-profile companies like Time Warner Cable and JCPenney. It would make him feel better if he knew somebody who was part of the process.

I had actually worked with Draxell and Schmidt before. In the summer after my second year of law school, I interned there under Steve Ogilvy, when he was a junior associate. And he gave me my first real grown-up job after graduation. I spent a couple of years there.

While I was talking I kept feeding Michael the basketball, and he shuffled around the key, taking sixteen-footers. One of his modes that you can see in his face is his consciously-reserving-judgment mode. Michael looks like his mother, he's a handsome kid, but somehow on him the effect is less glamorous and more puritanical. In high school I got the impression that girls were a bit scared of him; Miri said the same thing. Even the ones he went out with found him intense. He was always considerate, always happy to listen and talk, very sympathetic, but you could never tell what he actually thought about you, and after a while that makes him hard to take. Even for his father.

Eventually he said, "What kind of allegations?"

"Inappropriate workplace stuff. Comments on women's bodies in the office—mostly flattering comments. He said to a pregnant woman that maybe they could arrange for her to step aside for All-Star weekend, which was in Denver that year. Just to give her a break, he said. That's the kind of thing. He's clearly somebody who makes people around him uncomfortable. Then there are the racial allegations, which is what's actually driving this. On at least five occasions he's been heard using the N-word. He claims he was just quoting other people, reporting

34

conversations. Remember, this is over a period of almost twenty years."

"What's the right number of times to use the N-word in twenty years?" Michael asked. "Less than five?"

"Don't be a wiseass," I said. He had stopped shooting the basketball. We were just standing around.

"So what was your role in all this?"

"Marginal. I gave them some case law, but there's not a lot of precedent for sanctioning NBA owners. That's not really the point of this story."

He waited and eventually I said, "I don't know if you saw it in the news. The report came out and recommended a one-year suspension and a fine of fifteen million dollars. That's what the league decided. But the PR so far has been fairly disastrous. Anyway, if you look hard enough my name is on the report."

"So?"

"This is not a good time for me, I mean, at the law school. We've got a new dean, Dinah Shaw. I voted against her, which I don't think she holds against me but is just an indication of how we stand. Last year I had an issue with a couple of students—I teach a class on hate crime, which always provokes strong reactions. For some reason they decided to take it up with the dean. She's very . . . she tends to take the students' side. Nothing happened but if they connect my name to the Kirkland investigation, which they will . . . I don't see how I can avoid it now; it's just a matter of time."

"So what are you going to do?"

"Before we went to the Cape I talked to Dinah. She was perfectly reasonable, and also of course completely spineless. In the end we agreed I should take a leave of absence until the whole thing blows over. At least for the upcoming academic year. They're calling it an early sabbatical, though I'm only getting paid for one term."

"So when Miri goes, you guys . . . you're free agents."

"Sure."

"What did Mom say?"

"I haven't told her yet."

He didn't ask why not, but he took another shot and let me chase down the ball. I said to him, coming back, "We don't really communicate at that level anymore."

"What level is that? Does Miri know?"

"She's got enough on her plate."

"So why are you telling me?"

"I don't know, Michael. Because I'm not cut out for living a totally secret life. Can you understand that?"

"Sure, I understand. I just don't know what you expect me to do. Do you want me to tell Mom?"

"Give me a little time. I'll figure something out."

Before we left, I had to make three straight—this was my comfort routine. As a kid, that meant three-pointers, but these days sixteen- to eighteen-footers are enough. Still, it took a few minutes. The sun was going down behind the hoop; you couldn't really see the basket. But then a couple dropped in, and a third after that, with just a flick of the net, and for much of the way home I'm still the kid who feels like, that's the last thing I did. Whatever else is going on, the last thing I did was make three straight.

Michael put his hand on my shoulder. "I'm sorry, Dad."

"She isn't always sympathetic . . . she thinks I like picking fights. I know I have to tell her, but when I do, she'll blame me. She feels ashamed to be connected to someone with my opinions."

"Well, you like picking fights."

"Not really. That's not what it feels like. You reach a certain age and realize, the things you used to take for granted, that everybody you knew and liked agreed on, nobody agrees with you anymore about those things."

"You're on the wrong side of history."

"I guess that's true."

And then he said, because he's my son, and can't help himself: "For what it's worth, I don't think you should have gotten involved in the investigation."

"It's my job to think about this stuff."

"That's fine, but you should maybe think differently."

"You know what I find shameful. A number of players, and not just players, but coaches and front-office people, when the stories came out about Kirkland, immediately distanced themselves. They pretended to be shocked; they called for him to sell the team. And many of these people he either hired or drafted and would have considered himself to have a good personal relationship with. You know how many people said, humans are complicated, they're contradictory, they have good and bad sides, they say things

37

they shouldn't, they make mistakes, but that doesn't mean you give up on them. You know how many people in the organization said something like that? Nobody. Not one."

"I don't think you understand the opportunity here," Michael said. "You're still thinking about all this as if what we need are slight adjustments; you haven't understood the moment. This is a chance for a complete reset, which is also a basic acknowledgment of how bad things have been—on race and gender—for a very long time."

"I understand, believe me. I lived through more of it than you have."

"And by the way, if he hired or drafted them . . . do you really expect people in that situation can be honest with you? Or that what you have with them is in any meaningful sense a 'personal' relationship? Because if he thought that, that was his first mistake."

"Of course these are personal relationships. Just because there's a power dynamic, that doesn't mean . . ."

But by this point we were walking up the driveway. Dinner was on the table; Amy had lit candles. It was Miri's second-to-last night.

The next day, the Pritzkers came to lunch—friends from the synagogue. They had just gotten back from Fort Lauderdale and were more or less in the same boat as us: their daughter, Jessica, was about to go to Brown. Jess and Miri went to elementary school together and used to be close, at least in the way that the kids of family friends are sometimes close.

Enough to hang out uncomplainingly while their parents got drunk in the afternoon. But then the Pritzkers sent Jess to middle school in the city. She went to Dalton, which at least according to Amy explains why she got into Brown, which has an acceptance rate of under 8 percent, while Miri went to Scarsdale High and got into Carnegie Mellon, where the rate is closer to 18 percent.

Even at the time, Amy complained that we should be sending Miri private. For some reason, she didn't worry as much about Michael—boys, she said, don't care if they come across as nerds. But for girls the social pressure is a big distraction. Her mother gave her a Brearley education (I always hated this way of putting it), and she wanted to do the same for her daughter.

"But you were miserable."

"You know why that is, Tom. It had nothing to do with the school."

"You said to me you hated girls' schools because girls at that age are horrible people. That's what you said to me, when I asked you about female friends."

"We were dating, I was trying to sound interesting. Anyway, we can always send her to Dalton."

"Who's going to pay for it?" I asked.

It was around this time that I got an offer from Debevoise and Plimpton, one of the more progressive white-shoe firms. I had done some consulting work for them, and one thing led to another. Anyway, Amy wanted me to take the job.

"You understand what that means?" I told her. "Hundred-hour weeks, going into the office on a Sunday. No summers at the Cape, etc."

"*We* can still go," she said, meaning her and the kids, but she was only kidding. "All you do is complain about the law school. It's a dead end; I always thought you were more ambitious than that."

She used to say things like that to me, like a woman to a man. I almost took the job, just to please her—this was maybe five years after the affair with Zirsky. We were getting along better for a while; we were sleeping together again. But I didn't and so she sometimes blamed me for the way Miri turned out. Which is pretty great, if you ask me.

Except that Friday Miri had made other arrangements. She was hanging out with one of her old bandmates and didn't tell us. Then the Pritzkers came, and Jessica too, who wore a dress and flats and very smooth professional makeup and looked like Elizabeth Montgomery from *Bewitched*, cute and blonde and helpful. She pretended not to mind that Miri was out. The Pritzkers had brought a bottle of Pol Roger to celebrate our daughters' achievements, but since Miri wasn't there, we raised a glass to Jessica instead.

So for the rest of the afternoon Amy had to suppress feelings of disappointment and irritation. Jessica was more like the kind of daughter she thought she'd have.

But Chrissie Pritzker was also a good friend to Amy, even if I suspected she knew about the Zirsky business while it was going on. Afterward, though, when everything went to shit, she was a real help to Amy, which even at the time I was grateful for. Though it's also true she was maybe one of those women who derives secret energy from the troubles of her friends. Her husband, Dick, was a perfectly good guy, about six-two, fat and healthy. He worked for an online tech platform, I don't really know what he did.

We had bagels and eggs in the sun room, which had French doors opening out to the yard. So if you wanted you could take a plate of food onto the lawn. It was funny to see Michael talking to Jessica. He always acts like it's beneath him to notice the prettiness of girls, that's not how he thinks about people. But still I heard him asking her about Brown, and what she wanted to major in, and who her roommates were.

"I remember when I got to Swarthmore," he said. "I didn't know what hit me. I thought everybody was having the time of their lives except me."

"Oh no!" Jessica put her hand on his arm.

So people sat around all day, drinking. Dick is one of those guys I can talk sports with and not much else, which is fine by me. He had read about the Kirkland story, so we talked about that. Various players around the league had condemned his punishment as much too light; the NBA commissioner came in for a certain amount of flak. Which is all part of the show, I said. Part of an orchestrated campaign for getting rid of Kirkland. Right now they're just piling on the pressure.

Amy said, "Tom loves to stand up for racists. He teaches a whole class on it."

"That's not really true. I teach a class on hate crime."

Michael gave me a look, but I shook my head.

At three o'clock Miri came home. We could hear the front door, and Amy called out, "Who's there? Oh look, it's Miri. Miri's come back. She's decided to join us."

She stood in the doorway, between the old house and the extension.

"Let me just get changed."

"Come say hello to your old friends. They brought you champagne. Except maybe we drank it all."

"I just need to use the bathroom."

"You can come in for a minute and say hello," Amy said.

"I'll just be a second."

By the time Miri came down again the tone of the afternoon had changed. Amy let go a little. Sometimes if she was unhappy and drunk, the drink overrode the unhappiness, and she seemed in a good mood, but you could see underneath it too.

Dick asked me how I knew so much about the Nuggets story, and I mentioned the report. Also, my old friend Brian Palmetto, who I'd spoken to on the phone a few days before. When Kirkland sells his stake, Brian told me, I'll have to resign—there's no way new ownership will want to keep me. Even though I honestly don't know what I did wrong. Amy never liked Brian, for understandable reasons. There was a period, shortly after we started going out, when Brian tried to persuade me to move to California. This was still at a time in our twenties when your friends act like your loyalty to them is

42

deeper than any relationship. He was working as player/coach on a start-up league based in LA—hanging out at the gym all day, making three grand a month during the season. I actually flew out to take a look, but that's another story.

So when Brian's name came up, Amy said, "Good riddance." This is not how she talked about people sober, even people she didn't like.

"There's nothing in the report that reflects on him."

"I'm sorry, I just don't believe that if you have a sexist culture at an organization, Brian Palmetto is not part of the problem."

"You don't really know him anymore," I said.

After lunch it was the heat of the day, low 90s, and Amy brought out blankets and chairs so we could lie on the lawn. This was part of her Naftali charm, they were good at making occasions. She said to Jessica, "Come here and tell me about Brown. What's happening to your boyfriend? Are you staying together? Miri decided she wants a clean break."

So Miri went over to join them. They were sitting on one of the blankets. Amy when she wasn't drinking had to put her glass of champagne down carefully. She took off her shoes too, and stretched out her legs in the grass.

My back isn't great these days; Dick and I stayed on our feet. But I don't like direct sunlight on my head—there isn't the covering there used to be. At some point Amy turned her attention back to me.

"Why isn't he drinking? Why isn't he drinking?" she said. "He's letting me do all the drinking."

"You know he doesn't feel great," Miri told her.

"He doesn't even sit down anymore, he just stands there. He's always walking around."

"If I sit down I can't always get up."

"He's just getting ready to walk out on me."

"Nobody's walking out on you, Mom."

"You are."

Then Miri got mad. "Oh my God." They both had short tempers. Sometimes I even felt left out when they went at each other like this.

"Ask him," Amy said. "Just ask him." Eventually in her hostess voice she turned to Chrissie and Dick, "I'm sorry to bring out all our . . . unmentionables in public."

"Look, we're old friends. This is a stressful time."

"It's just that trying to get him to talk about anything when we're alone is like getting blood from a stone."

Not long after this the party broke up; Jessica still had some packing to do. Me too, Miri said. Amy for a second had a hard time getting onto her feet. I hated seeing her like this. She didn't much like it either. "Give me a hand," she said quietly so I came over to pull her up. For a minute she stood leaning against me.

"You see, he loves me."

"Of course he does," Chrissie said.

"He's just so cold cold cold." She started pretending to hit me in the chest and I held on, partly to stop her but also to keep her up. "I just don't know what I'm going to do when it's just us."

"You don't have to do anything," Chrissie said.

After they left, Amy went to lie down and Miri and Michael and I cleaned up. Nobody said much, except that Miri said, "Jesus."

"You okay?"

"Maybe it makes it easier."

We brought the blankets in and loaded the dishwasher and threw away a lot of food. Michael was flying back to LA, and the rest of us were driving up to Pittsburgh, where Amy and I planned to stay the night with our old Somerville pal Sam Tierney, who was now a professor at Pitt. So there was no point letting things like a plate of lox stink up the fridge.

"What are you doing now? Packing?"

And she said, "*Call of Duty*?"

This is one of the games we used to play together, senior year, after she finished her homework. She said it calmed her down before bed, which Amy didn't understand at all—you just go around shooting things. I found it helped me relax, too. A lot of short-term goals. But then Michael wanted to play, so I left them to it.

"Isn't she a little young for you?" Miri asked her brother. The PlayStation was in the TV den, next to the dining room. You had to unhook and hook various cables.

"Who?"

"Jess."

"Young for what?"

"Gross," Miri said.

"I think I'll lie down too," I announced and went upstairs.

The bedroom was only half-dark when I opened the door. Six o'clock summer sunlight glowed between the curtains. I couldn't tell if Amy was asleep but then she said, "I'm sorry," and I lay down next to her with my clothes on. She was under the blanket but I lay on top. "I got drunk. I'm so ashamed, you don't have to say anything."

"I wasn't going to."

We lay there for a minute, and then Amy said, "What's she doing now?" She sounded wide awake.

"Playing computer games."

"Alone?"

"With Michael."

"Well, okay." Amy didn't like computer games. She said no one in her family ever played them.

Whenever I lie down I feel the blood slowly build up in my head; it's very strange, like a hand squeezing my neck and another one pressing down on my face. After a while you get used to it, but you also think, if you stand up, stand up in stages.

"Do you think she's a lesbian?" Amy asked. We were just voices, really, staring at the ceiling.

"What are you talking about?"

"Meeting up with Avery like that, on her last day. Do you think something's going on?"

"They had lunch. No, I don't think she's a lesbian."

"I don't understand why she broke up with Jim."

"Maybe she didn't like him that much."

46

More silence; I closed my eyes.

"We were going through her emails," Amy said eventually, "to see if she'd remembered everything, and I saw a message from Mrs. Griffin. I said, what's that, but she didn't want to show me. Anyway, it was a very nice email, extremely complimentary. When you get to CMU, it said, you should look up my friend Kathy Myers, who teaches in the drama department and organizes all the productions. She gave her an email address. So I said to Miri, that's nice, have you written to her? And she said, Mom, just leave it. I'm not even there yet, give me a break. And I said, of course, that's fine, I just want to know if you're going to write to her, because this could be a real opportunity, and she said, probably not. I said, why not, and she said, I don't want to act anymore."

"So she doesn't want to act."

"You don't understand her at all. She's being defensive and she's being defensive because her confidence took a hit. Because of Jim."

"That's not the sense I get."

"Tom, she's talented, it's one thing she's actually good at. She's very natural. That's not easy. Not everybody has that."

"But she doesn't want to do it. I don't know. Maybe when she gets there she'll change her mind."

"That's your answer to everything, isn't it. You always think everything is fine."

"No, I don't."

"I don't want to lie here with you," Amy said.

Then I was alone in the room, thinking, if you fall asleep now, you won't be able to sleep later.

When I woke up again, the room was dark, and somewhere, downstairs, someone was shouting. I couldn't tell how much time had passed, maybe an hour. I felt knocked on the head. Then another voice came into it and I realized it was Miri and her mother. You should get up, I thought, you should go downstairs, and after a minute, I did, feeling unsteady and holding on to the bannister.

"What's going on?"

Michael was there too. He said, "It's probably better you stay out of it."

"What time is it?"

I had left my watch on the bedside table, I don't like to sleep with a wristwatch on. Lately I'd been waking up with swollen hands.

"Nine o'clock."

"Shouldn't she be packing?"

"That's part of what they're fighting about."

There was no particular time we had to leave in the morning, but I wanted to make an early start. It's a seven-hour drive from Scarsdale to Pittsburgh. Also, we had to load up the car, not just with her suitcases but any dorm-room stuff she wanted to take, and then unload it again at the other end, so she had time to make her room feel nice and homey before she spent the first night. I tried to say as much but Amy said it didn't matter anyway, because she wasn't going—if Miri didn't want her to come along, she wouldn't come.

Miri said, "Of course I don't want you to come if all you do is criticize me."

"God, you're sensitive. I was just making a suggestion."

"Maybe it is better if Dad takes her," Michael said. He was talking to his mother.

"Did I say something wrong? Did I do something wrong?"

"No, you're both as bad as each other. But it might be better tomorrow just to lower the emotional temperature. Say goodbye in the morning and keep it simple."

Amy suddenly burst into tears. "You know he's going to leave me, right? You know that, don't you? He's been planning it for a long time."

"Nobody's planning anything, she's just going to college. All of this is normal. Everything you're feeling is normal." And Michael, as he said this, kept stroking the side of her arm.

"I don't know what I'm going to do without you either," Amy said.

"Call me on the phone."

"Aren't you going to say something?" She was looking at me.

"I'm just trying to figure out what the hell's going on."

"You know what's going on," Amy said.

But in the end we all sat down in front of the TV and watched a *Simpsons* rerun. It was from one of the later series and not particularly funny, but Miri laughed anyway. That's something she could do—whatever mood she was in, she could snap out of it and act like everything was fine. And by the time we said goodnight, maybe it was. Amy even went into her bedroom to kiss her and turn out the lights, and after a few minutes came out again and put her arms around me.

"You don't have to say anything," she said again.

It still seemed amazing to me sometimes that this girl who, when I first saw her at Ethan Konchar's party, seemed too pretty for me to even talk to her, had become this person with such complicated resentments and dependencies directed at me. I don't think I was worth it.

Amy woke up early to make potato pancakes, which was Miri's favorite breakfast as a kid. She had worked off most of her hangover the previous evening but still had a headache, which was maybe also meteorological, because a summer storm blew in overnight and the light outside was a kind of fraught gray, overcast but bright. I lay in bed for half an hour listening to her in the kitchen, which was directly below our bedroom, then went downstairs and watched Amy cook, sitting half-asleep on one of the bar stools.

In the mornings, my face was always swollen with fluid, and my eyes leaked like a sponge if you pressed them. Amy hated looking at me like this so usually looked away. Then around eight I went up to get the kids.

There's a phrase that used to go through my thoughts— the heavy tread of middle age on the family stairs. Moving around the house I sounded more and more like my dad, with an oof in each step.

So we had a last family breakfast, then packed the car.

In our garage we had all kinds of junk, a functional microwave, several radios and CD players, drawers of abandoned cutlery, and a big plastic trash can with old blankets, from our grad school rental in Porter Square, and our first married apartment in the city, which we sublet from Amy's mother's sorority friend, in Yorkville, on the poorer side of the Upper East Side. Miri took the microwave and one of the blankets, also a little three-shelf bookcase and one of the cutlery sets. The car filled up; Amy kept trying to bring out more things, a vase, pillows and throws from the living-room sofa.

"I just don't want you to be cold. It gets very cold in Pennsylvania."

"Mom, it's the same latitude as New York." Eventually Miri said, "This is stupid, you should just come along."

"But I haven't even packed."

"What do you need to pack for?"

"We're staying overnight with Sam Tierney. I told your father, I just want to drive home afterward."

"That's a fourteen-hour drive, there and back," I said.

We were standing in the driveway; overnight, thousands of leaves and twigs had fallen onto the road and the front yards. There was still a lot of movement in the trees.

"So pack an overnight bag and come. It'll take you five minutes."

And Amy actually went upstairs. After a while I said, "Michael, why don't you go see what's going on." And then to Miri: "Do you want her to come?"

"Of course I want her . . . but not if she's going to freak out on me."

"I'm sorry to say I might freak out on you a bit too."

"That's not your style."

Then Michael and Amy walked out together, and Michael said, "She's going to stay. Clean break. My flight's not till six; I can stick around and have lunch."

"I just don't think I can sit there in the car for seven hours and not stress everybody out. You're better off just the two of you."

"Don't do that, don't put this on me," Miri said.

But they hugged in the driveway and for a minute Amy wouldn't let go. It made me feel funny to look at them; I don't know what you're supposed to feel. Even at fifty-two Amy was still the more conventionally attractive woman, and wore skinny Veronica Beard jeans and clogs and a linen shirt. Whereas Miri dressed like the boys I went to high school with, who didn't care what they looked like. She had a Mickey Mouse sweatshirt on, which was two sizes too big, and other than that you couldn't really see what she was wearing. But if you had to bet on one of them in a fight, or even just . . . which of these people is going to have a happy life, you'd bet on Miri.

At some level everything you feel or think is a kind of taking sides.

Then Michael hugged her and she got in the car. I was already waiting in the driver's seat. Miri rolled down her window and Michael said, "Don't worry about the next couple weeks. Nobody's having that much fun, I don't care what they say."

Amy asked me, "When will I see you again?"

"Tomorrow late, unless I stay another night. I'll call you from the road."

Then I reversed out of the drive, and they stood there until we couldn't see them anymore.

In the end, the reason she told me about Zach Zirsky was because they broke up and she needed somebody to talk to about it. Somebody who loved her. We had a rough few weeks. I was on the search committee for a new dean, along with Dinah Shaw, who backed Tony Akbar, the guy who eventually got the job and later made way for Dinah herself. It was a very contentious time at the law school. Colleagues kept coming into my office, saying their piece, and expecting me to take certain public positions. The president of the student bar association, who had a seat on the committee, was actually in my contracts seminar and strongly supported Akbar, as did most of the student body. Akbar and I got along fine but his scholarship was second-rate. I worried that as a dean he would push the law school in a direction I didn't like, and where my own work was less valued, which is what ended up happening. Anyway, it made the meetings awkward, game-planning beforehand what I should say and wondering afterward how whatever I *did* say had played with various factions in the room.

Maybe it was a useful distraction. Sometimes when I got back to my office I closed the door and turned the lights off and lay down on the two-seater under the window. But Amy kept calling me. We found it easier to talk over the phone.

It was late summer; the days were getting shorter. After work I'd walk across the Park to Fifth Avenue and down to Grand Central and then catch the train to Scarsdale. Michael would still be up when I got home but Miri was usually in bed. She liked to stay awake until I kissed her goodnight, so when I walked in the front door I went straight upstairs.

Michael was old enough, he figured out what was going on. He overheard us fighting, or maybe he knew anyway. Amy in those days was emotionally very exposed; she might have told him. They were very close. But it meant I couldn't really face him, which was not his fault. I thought he thought, if you were a real man you wouldn't put up with this shit, though of course he never said anything like that. It's what *my* dad would have said. The three of us had a conversation where Amy and I basically explained, married people go through ups and down just like any other friends, it doesn't mean we don't love each other. People do things they shouldn't, which they regret, and then you have to forgive them. But you know, it's not easy. They have to forgive themselves, too. None of this has anything to do with you.

But Miri was just six years old. So when I sat with her I didn't have to pretend with her or feel any shame.

Which meant we never had this conversation and even now, twelve years later, I didn't know what she knew or what she remembered from this period of her childhood. And now she was leaving. We drove through White Plains and over the river, through Nyack and then into New Jersey. I let Miri choose the music; for the first fifty miles we didn't talk much. I figured it's a seven-hour drive, there's plenty of time for conversation. But I also had this urge to explain myself to her, and for her to explain herself to me, before she went off. For the past six years, since Michael left for Swarthmore, Miri was stuck in the house alone with her two inadequate parents. And if anybody kept us together, she did. This is obviously the wrong pressure to put on a kid, but for most of that time she probably qualified as my best friend, even though there are clearly limits to what you tell your daughter and what she tells you.

By the way, I'm glad to admit she wouldn't say the same about me.

The music she was into was eighties synthy stuff, songs like "Tainted Love" and bands like the Eurythmics. She liked them in a retro ironic way, because they had amped-up sounds and emotions, which she could pretend to have and make fun of at the same time. Technically, I guess, this was my musical era, but I was more of a Springsteen fan or even John Cougar Mellencamp, what Miri called corny, depressing white-guy music, with a slow banging beat and strummy guitar. But, you know, where the basic goal is still authenticity. Good road-trip music, especially if you're taking 80 West through Pennsylvania. Whatever, I let her play what she wanted. Like "Chains of Love," which I remember hating when it came out, around the time of my high school prom, where I did *not* have a good time.

This is the kind of thing I could talk to her about. At the back of my mind I had made a promise to myself not to have the conversation about her mother, even if in the moment it seemed appropriate.

Just before Altoona we stopped for lunch at a Cracker Barrel. She had pancakes, I ordered the fried chicken, and while the food was cooking I asked her about Michael. She said, what about Michael.

"How's he doing? He doesn't really talk to me about personal stuff."

"I think he wants a girlfriend."

"Does he have somebody in mind?"

Her pancakes arrived, with breakfast sausage, eggs over easy and homestyle fried potatoes. There was a syrup pot on the table and she poured a thick gloop over half the plate. I thought, if Amy were here, she'd say something, but I didn't say anything. It was three in the afternoon and we'd been eating crap all day. This is one of those days that exist outside the lines, where nothing really counts.

"Betty or something. Betsey. She's a little older than he is. He said she has a hinterland."

"What does that mean?"

"Before she went to grad school, she worked as a vet. In like, Montana."

"Well, that's the hinterland. How old is old?"

"Not old. Like thirty. He worries that maybe she's not as smart as he is, but then he thought, maybe it doesn't matter. In other ways she makes him feel pretty dumb."

"That doesn't sound good."

"Not dumb but like, he still has a lot to learn."

"He told you all this?"

"He doesn't like to give me advice about my life unless he's willing to talk about whatever he's got going on."

"What kind of advice?"

But then her phone rang, which she had out on the table and was thumbing through even while she ate. "Hey, Mom," she said. She was mostly finished anyway; I don't think she was actually that hungry. All the food on her plate had gotten mixed up and cold.

"Does she want to talk to me?"

But Miri ignored me, so I got up and went to the restroom. I took a leak and washed my face and stood in front of the mirror, looking at my face. To see how swollen it was. Miri, when she came down to breakfast, sometimes called me Puff Daddy. I called her P Daughter, it was part of the routine. I didn't mind, because it meant she didn't take it seriously. I didn't want her to worry. She thought it was just a middle-aged thing. And maybe it was, because as the day wore on my face drained and I started to look like myself again. So every time I saw a mirror I looked to see what age and condition of person was staring back at me.

After that I spent a minute checking my phone. I don't

like to take it out in front of the kids. There were various law school emails I didn't have to deal with, one of the advantages of being on forced leave, and a missed call from Brian Palmetto. At first I thought it was a butt call. You could hear airport noises in the background, the PA system announcing a gate change for the flight to San Diego, but then Brian's voice kicked in. "Hey, Tommy," he said. He sounded vaguely drunk. "I've got a business proposition for you. Give me a call. Somebody I think you should meet. Or don't worry about it, I'll call you." Then he said something to somebody else and hung up, and I was back in the restroom at Cracker Barrel, amid the brown tiles.

Miri was still on the phone when I came back. "Does she want to talk to me?"

"Do you want to talk to Dad?" she asked, and gave me the phone.

"Hey, Amy."

"Hey, Tom. How does she seem?"

"How do you seem?" I said to Miri.

"I seem amazing," she said.

"She's amazing."

"I'm sorry I'm not there. Michael just left."

"It's fine. Maybe it's simpler."

"I don't know that I can just sit here . . . I said I don't know if I can just sit here for the rest of the day. I'll go crazy."

"Call Chrissie."

"Thanks, you're a lot of help. I don't know what's wrong with me. I should have just come along."

"You wanted to make it easier for her to say goodbye."

"That's what I do. I make everything easy for everybody," and she hung up.

"Does she want to talk to me again?" Miri said, when I passed her the phone. But it was dead.

Later, after paying the bill, I asked her, "I don't understand, is Michael going out with this girl?"

"I think he wants to."

"I mean, has he made a move?"

"I think they have one of those friendships where they talk about their friendship a lot."

"That sounds like Michael."

We went out into the parking lot, where you could already hear the highway. You look at the parked cars and think, all these people have some reason to stop here on the way to somewhere else. This far inland there was no sign of the storm front, it was just a humid August day. Heavy trees grew up in picnic areas around the lot. A few people had let their dogs out to use the grass. We got back in the car.

"Is Mom all right?" Miri said, and I thought, don't go into it. That's what you decided.

"She'll be fine. It's an adjustment for us, too."

"But you'll be okay?"

She was looking at me, and I wondered if Michael had said something.

"Don't worry about us. That's not your job anymore."

For another second she looked at me, then looked away.

I pulled onto the interstate, and then it was just . . . the usual endless stream. You become a part of the pattern. We had another two hours to go before Pittsburgh. Miri started painting her nails, each one a different color—black, red, yellow, green—sitting with her boots on the dashboard and the polish lined up in the cup holder next to me.

"Is that how you plan to show up at college?"

"It relaxes me," she said.

"Just don't make a mess. You know how your mother feels about the upholstery."

I figured it was something for her to do so she didn't have to talk, but after a while I started talking anyway.

"So what was his advice?"

"What do you mean?"

"You said Michael wanted to give you some advice."

"I don't know, you know what he's like."

At least while she did her nails, I could take over the music; she sat with her fingers in the air. So I started flicking through radio stations, until I got to WDVE, Home of the Pittsburgh Steelers, where "Pancho and Lefty" was playing, followed by "If I Leave Here Tomorrow," and "Cowgirl in the Sand," which saw us through another six or seven miles.

"Your mother thinks that maybe you're a lesbian."

"I wish," Miri said. Then, after a minute, "She doesn't really think that."

"She just can't understand why you broke up with Jim."

"I don't like to tell you guys things that might make you mad at him."

"Why should we be mad?"

Around us, on both sides of the four-lane highway, were low hills, covered in thick woods. Not bad country, where it's easy to feel, this is still a continent where you can start again.

Eventually she said, "He thought we should see other people. He wanted to stay together but he thought we should be free to . . . he thought I should have the full college experience. He wanted to have the whole Harvard thing, whatever that means."

"What an asshole."

"That's why I didn't want to tell you. Please don't tell Mom."

"Why not?"

"She loves Jim. I don't want her to be disappointed. Also, like, of course you should have the whole Harvard experience, if that's what you want. That's why people go to Harvard."

"But it sounds like that's not really what you wanted."

"No."

It's easy to talk in the car, because you don't have to say anything. The miles drift by anyway. And what I was thinking about was . . . Miri at Boulder Brook Field, playing soccer on a Saturday morning. She was one of those girls who is taller than everybody for about two years, then gets stuck at whatever height she's going to be (five-eight) when she's twelve years old and spends the rest of her teenage years watching everyone catch up. But when she first started playing she was bigger and faster and had about twice as much energy as the other kids. She played midfield, she was a good organizer, and you could actually hear her from the sidelines, shouting encouragement. For a while I used to think, okay, you're going to have to deal with this, you're going to have to arrange your life around it to a certain extent, that your daughter has real athletic talent, but somehow without any big dramatic failure or falling out it just turned into something she did on Saturday mornings, until she got to high school and quit.

"I sometimes worry that you're not as . . . gung ho as you used to be about things. Which is definitely how I feel, so I don't blame you."

"That's a funny word," she said.

"What?"

And she started playing around with it. "Don't act like no gung ho."

"I'm sorry," I said, because she was trying to change the conversation.

"About what."

"That you have to deal with stuff like this."

"We had to break up eventually. It's probably better to get it over with. By the way, in case you're wondering, you look normal again."

"Thank you."

"I mean your face."

"I know what you mean."

"That's something else Michael got on my case about. He says you need to see a doctor."

"I've seen several doctors."

"That's what I told him."

"I'm just a middle-aged guy, getting older."

"That's what I said. You're not going to drop dead on me, are you?"

"I don't have any plans to."

"Because . . ." and she turned away for a minute. "I'm sorry," she said. "I'm just a little nervous."

"Now you've got me going," I said.

"Don't you start."

"Who am I going to watch *Friends* with?"

Because when the schools shut in March of 2020, this is what we used to do. Around six o'clock, Amy made cocktails, and we all sat down to watch TV. Sometimes I gave Miri a sip. For a while we tried to pick a different movie each night, but nobody could agree, and Miri just wanted comfort TV, reruns and sitcoms, and since I didn't really care, she got her way. But Amy had snobby opinions, she had a whole Naftali thing about pop culture, and eventually it was just Miri and me. We worked our way through all ten seasons, watching the show get steadily worse. People turning into caricatures, but maybe this is what happens to people.

Amy used to get dinner ready and finish off what was left in the cocktail shaker. Sometimes I fell asleep on the couch. I wasn't sleeping well in the night, so when it was time to eat I had to be woken up. After a while you can get nostalgic about anything.

"Mom," Miri said.

"You know she doesn't watch that stuff."

"Anyway, we've seen them all now. You didn't even really like it."

Eventually we hit the outskirts of the Pittsburgh conurbation, Delmont, Export, Murrysville; there were traffic lights in the road. We kept stopping and starting; the atmosphere tightened. Less than an hour to go and then we'd be there.

You could see Miri almost physically reminding herself to be interested in someone else's life. At one point she said, "When does your teaching start?"

"I don't know, a few weeks."

"You don't know?"

"I'm not that worried about it."

Maybe this is stupid, maybe Michael said something to her; but the effort had been made, she let it go. Also, she's the kind of loving daughter who doesn't like to think about anything unhappy in her father's life.

"You changed your mind?" I said, and Miri looked at her hands. She had taken out nail polish remover and started cleaning her nails.

"It was just something to do."

"You excited by what comes next?"

"Sure," she said.

Downtown Pittsburgh was upon us now, the wide half-busy avenues, handsome and civic and a little gloomy. After that I was too busy following Google Maps to pay much attention to the emotional temperature. Miri sat with her feet on the dashboard, looking out of the window. This city she had visited once before was about to become a permanent four-year landmark in her life story, and in the face of that fact you're kind of helplessly the person you were beforehand.

When we parked in the street outside Donner House, one of the freshman dorms, it took her a minute to lace up her big DMs. I always needed a minute to stand up anyway, to wait for my head to clear, and leaned against the door after getting out until the wave passed. Sometimes it was all right, sometimes not, but after three hours sitting driving I had a real zinger, a black rush like a train coming down a subway tunnel, including the noise. But it passed. The car was full of crap—empty Bugles wrappers and soda bottles, Kleenex tissues smeared with nail polish. I tried to clean up a little while she got ready, but there weren't any trash cans on the sidewalk or next to the building or on the municipal lawns out front, so I just carried this stuff around in my hand.

Miri was pulling her suitcase out of the trunk, which was also full of boxes and blankets, the old microwave, etc.

"I could use some help here," she said. And then, "Dad, just put that stuff down, it doesn't matter."

"I can't find a trash can."

"Who cares?"

"Well, what am I supposed to do with it?" She looked at me from the road, and I stood on the sidewalk looking back. For some reason I had lost the ability to make decisions.

"Just throw it in the car."

So that's what I did, on the floor of the passenger seat.

It was after seven o'clock, still light out, humid and overcast. We'd had a late lunch so I wasn't particularly hungry, but the evening had that slightly adrift feeling, where there's no plan for dinner and you still don't know exactly where you're going to sleep. At some point I had to get in touch with Sam Tierney. But if Miri wanted to go out for a late bite, I wanted to be available for that, too. But she didn't want to. It took us an hour to find the keys and carry all the boxes and bags from the street to her room on the second floor, which overlooked the lawn and the car and the road. Donner was one of those seventies-style buildings that look like the architectural plans, but dirtier.

The room was fine, though. Her roommate, Susan Shapiro (they'd spoken on the phone), must have moved in earlier but wasn't around. The first thing Miri did was make her bed; she's better at that kind of thing than I am. A lot of school camping trips. She seemed all right. I was just standing there, thinking, this is where you have to live now, baby girl. But going back and forth from the car kept me busy for a while. Then when I walked down the long windowless hall for the fourth time I heard people talking, and I listened for a minute outside before going in.

Miri was in semi-public mode, cheerful and competent.

I said, "Can I take you guys out for dinner?"

But Susan had already eaten and Miri just wanted to

settle in. "I'm too wired to eat anyway," she said.

"You have to eat."

But she still had the box of Entenmann's and Susan said there was milk in the fridge. "That's a good balanced diet," she said—I mean, Susan said it. I thought, maybe it's time to clear out and let the next stage begin. For both of us.

Miri walked me to the car, to say goodbye. She put her arm around my waist and we moved a little awkwardly, hip to hip. It was nine o'clock by now. The old-fashioned globe lamps were lit beside the walkways, and the sprinkler system had kicked in; the grass smelled wet. I had a sense of undigested emotional material, which is really just a disconnect between the totally normal passage of time you happen to be in and the totally normal passage of time that is about to follow, after which everything will be permanently different.

"What are you going to do now," Miri said.

"I told you, I'm staying with Sam Tierney. We'll probably get something to eat. He's a bit of a night owl."

"And after that, you're going home?"

"What do you mean, after that?"

"Tomorrow."

"Where else would I go?" But I couldn't tell if she meant anything by it. "If you need anything in the morning, just let me know."

"I'm sure I'll be fine."

"Even if you just want someone to take you out to breakfast. Susan too."

"That's sweet," she said. And then she hugged me and waited on the sidewalk until I drove away.

II

I knew Sam Tierney through Ethan Konchar, Amy's old boyfriend. Ethan and I met at Pomona but didn't get to know each other until senior year, when we joined Mufti. I don't want to talk about Mufti. It's one of those secret society things people sign up for when they think their bright college days are slipping away. We played witty practical jokes around campus: it wasn't really my scene. But I liked Ethan. He's extremely smart but also more generally one of those people you meet at these institutions who is like some NBA-level example of realized human potential. He could cook, even as an undergrad; if you got into a political argument with him, it turned out he had access to reliable inside information that would genuinely change your mind. He also lettered on the Ultimate Frisbee team and ran a steady six-minute mile, so it was a good idea not to go jogging with him.

After Pomona he did a PhD in computer science at Harvard. His real subject was artificial intelligence. I got into BU to study Twentieth-Century American Lit. Since I didn't know anybody else in town, I looked him up. Ethan lived on the middle floor of one of those ugly Victorian triple-deckers you get in Somerville, where every neighborhood street seems to lead back into itself. Sam Tierney was his roommate. He was at Harvard too, but doing English like me, and sat around the apartment in a Liberty of London bathrobe and leaving half-drunk cups of Ovaltine on every surface.

That's the thing about Sam—he was always around. If you needed somebody to do something with, like drive out to the new Trader Joe's, he would do it. At the same time he held in reserve his own vivid and peculiar sense that he was living some wonderful privileged life of the mind and surrounded by a cast of colorful characters, which . . . I don't know, maybe he was, maybe we were. Often, when I dragged him out to lunch, I had to wait while he got dressed. But he was always happy to be distracted. Whereas Ethan looked at you with this friendly air of expectation that whatever you were about to say was going to interest and amuse him. I'm not really up for that kind of pressure.

Amy practically lived with both of them before she went out with me. I think Ethan's attitude to their relationship was, if you're going to date someone at Harvard, go out with the most beautiful woman of your acquaintance, which he had now done. So when he got the fellowship in Göttingen he figured, okay, let's see what's next. I don't even mean that I disliked him for it. Personally, he was always very charming, which isn't, whatever people say, a superficial quality; but it also made me feel a little sorry for Amy. She was twenty-three and beginning to find out that certain guys, who weren't obviously awful or unreliable, would consider her to be part of their experience of the world.

Sam lived in Highland Park, where a lot of the professors live. It's only a fifteen-minute drive from Donner but I had to pull over a few blocks after saying goodbye to put the address in my phone.

I'd been to his house before, about ten years earlier. He bought it when his father died, just to deal with the inheritance, so he didn't fritter it away. But the house itself was much too big for him. Maybe at the time he thought he might get married, I don't know. But he still lived there alone, halfway up North Sheridan, near the Park. It looked like his place in Somerville, old and gloomy, with wide steps leading up to the front door under a pillared awning.

When I rang the bell, it took him a minute to answer. Then he stared at me a second before saying, "Hey, Tom."

He had a soft American voice, a radio voice, which had only gotten sweeter with age.

"You seem a little surprised."

"Not at all, not at all. But I thought you might be the Amazon guy. Come in."

There was a rather grand entrance hall, with a chandelier and more wide steps leading up to the second floor. I dumped my backpack next to the umbrella stand and felt like a college kid, coming to mow the lawn.

I asked him if he'd eaten already, and he said, "I don't know."

"You don't know?"

"It doesn't matter, I'm always happy to eat."

But it was too late to go out, so we ordered what he called mediocre acceptable Indian, and while we were waiting, opened a bottle of wine. I told him, I'm not really a big drinker right now, for various reasons, but by the end of the evening we'd gotten through two bottles of Sonoma Coast Pinot Noir.

Until the food arrived, we sat in the living room, which overlooked the front yard. It had a fireplace with a painted screen and a couple of bentwood armchairs on either side. There's no point going over the conversation in detail, but I can tell you what we talked about. I mentioned that I'd just dropped Miri off at school. At school, he said, and I had to explain that she was going to Carnegie Mellon. He hadn't taken in the reason for my staying over, which made me not want to talk about it much. But after a while you get over that kind of thing. He had his own private life, which I was also ignorant of.

When the doorbell rang I thought it was the food. But it was in fact the Amazon guy, who gave him a large soft package, which he left on the stairs. Then the curry came and we moved to the dining room.

At some point he asked me, how's the teaching, and I told him about my conversation with the dean.

"So what are you going to do?"

"I don't know, maybe look for consulting work. Try and make a lot of money."

"Do you want a lot of money?"

"It's something to want."

"Why don't you write that book?" It was one of Sam's romantic ideas that I should be a writer.

"What book?"

But he had already moved on. "It's only a matter of time," he said. "This is what I tell myself. Before they kick me out, too."

"What do you mean?"

"I'm a middle-aged white man who likes to teach dead white men. Eventually, in the ten or so hours a week I get paid to talk to twenty-year-olds, I'll say something that one of them takes a righteous objection to. Which wouldn't surprise me at all, I have many objectionable thoughts. If you stand up in front of kids you end up saying some of them. I don't have to tell you. And when that happens, do I expect the Chair to have my back? No, I do not."

"So what are you going to do?"

"Nothing. Enjoy it while it lasts. Look, my situation is different from yours. I don't have any family left to have to pretend to be ashamed in front of."

Amy called while we were eating. I thought it might be Miri so checked my phone and didn't have the heart not to answer it.

"We're just having dinner," I said.

"At ten o'clock?"

"It's been a long day."

"How's Miri?"

73

"Fine, she's fine. She kicked me out, she's happy. Can I call you later?"

"I don't know. I'm going to bed, I don't know what else to do."

"That was Amy," I said, after hanging up. "We've been having a fight about Miri."

We were sitting now at the old mahogany table in the dining room, where he also liked to work. There were papers pushed to one side, and plastic containers of food, gathering oil.

"Is that why she didn't come?"

"Who knows?"

At a certain age you start making conscious decisions about who you feel close enough to talk to, or maybe it's just something you learn how to do, it doesn't matter who with. "Anyway," I said. "Miri split up with her high-school boyfriend a few weeks ago. I said to Amy, she's just moving on, but Amy thinks it's a sign of something else. Like, she's giving up. There have been other . . . indicators. So I tried to talk to Miri about it in the car."

"What did she say?"

"Not much, she's eighteen years old. But sometimes I worry that it's filtered down from me."

"What do you mean, that you've given up?"

"That's what Amy thinks," I said.

Around eleven the doorbell rang again, and Sam said, "Excuse me a moment," so I sat in the dining room and picked at the food. It seemed a long time ago that Michael

74

and Amy waved us off in the road. I could hear him speaking to somebody in the hallway, a woman's voice, and then they both came in.

"I'd like to introduce you to a friend of mine," he said. I thought he was talking to her but he was talking to me. "Deborah Linden, she's doing her PhD in thing theory."

"What's that?"

"He pretends he doesn't understand it," Deborah said.

She was small and pretty, with straight long hair and a powdered face, where the makeup is like a mask that hides her actual face. She looked tired and young; I didn't know if I should get up.

"Are you hungry?" Sam was very solicitous. "We can heat something up."

"I ate on the plane."

Eventually she sat down and he poured her a glass of wine, which she didn't finish. She had just flown in from Austin after spending six weeks at the Harry Ransom Center, working on Jack London, of all people. "I expect you can tell from my tan."

"How did you like Austin?"

"I loved it," but I couldn't tell what she meant.

It was clear to me they wanted to be left alone, which was fine with me. At one point Sam said to her, "The pillow arrived," and she said, "The pillow?"

"Synthetic fiber."

"Thank you, Sam." They were formal and polite with each other, and finally I said, "Look, it's been a long day. I'm sorry to break up the party."

"Let me just show you your room."

On the way upstairs he was clearly embarrassed. It was hard for me to associate him with anything dishonorable, but maybe it's also true his sense of honor had dated a little. He never talked to me about his girlfriends and I never asked him. The only thing he said was, "She hasn't always been treated well by the department. Her tastes are actually fairly conservative. You can more or less pick your bedroom . . ."

There were four or five on the second floor, but they seemed to run into each other; you couldn't always tell what was supposed to be hallway or dressing room. Sam slept at the front of the house so I chose one at the rear, which had a window onto the yard and a narrow carpeted bathroom on the landing outside. Back stairs led to the kitchen. I didn't ask him if the sheets were clean.

"Will you be all right?" he said, standing in the doorway. "Do you have everything you need?"

For three months we lived together, after Ethan moved to Göttingen. When I arrived in Boston, I rented a unit in one of BU's residence halls, which had a shared kitchen and bathroom, because it was cheap. But it was like living in a youth hostel or a three-star hotel for a couple of years. So when Sam needed a new roommate, I jumped, even if it was a little weird for Amy . . . who ended up changing boyfriends but somehow staying over in the same apartment. But anyway, for three months Sam and I were roommates, while important things were happening in my life.

"I'm fine. It's nice to see you," I said.

"I can't tell how you're doing but maybe we can talk more tomorrow. I've got a squash game in the morning but we can have lunch. When are you heading back?"

"I haven't made my mind up yet."

"So let's have lunch."

"Okay, good night," I said.

Then for the first time all day, apart from those fifteen minutes in the car after dropping Miri off, I was alone. There was an old jute rug on the floor that smelled like water damage so I opened the window, onto the summer night. The yard, in the half-light coming from a street lamp, looked dirty and yellow; it had a tennis court at the back. Sam used to play tennis with people; in grad school that was part of his social calendar. (It annoyed me because he usually beat me, even though I'm basically a better athlete. This is the advantage of going to prep school.) But the court seemed in bad shape. My vague sense, from the house and everything else, was that Sam hadn't fully inhabited his life—he lived like he was still renting. But what does that mean, who isn't.

I felt very low. Homeless. Miri was gone, Michael was in LA. I had no job to go back to. The bed was made but probably hadn't been changed in years; everything seemed dusty. But you go through the usual routine, you brush your teeth in the bathroom, you fold your clothes and lay them on the chair. The kitchen was underneath my room and I could hear Sam and Deborah talking, loading the dishwasher or making coffee, just a hum of conversation, no words.

Amy texted while I was in bed with the light off, looking at my phone. Are you awake, can I talk to you. So I called her in the dark, it was after midnight. Somehow there was an intimacy about lying there in the strange room with her on the other end of the technology that I hadn't felt in months.

"Sam has a girl over," I said.

"A girl?"

"One of the grad students. I don't know if he's actually supervising her, probably not."

"What's she like?"

"A lot of makeup. She didn't say much, she'd just gotten off a flight. Sam was funny around her, he seemed embarrassed."

"I don't want to talk about Sam," Amy said.

So we tried to talk about Miri. I described her room, I described her roommate. I said I offered to take them out to dinner, I offered to get them breakfast in the morning, but she just wanted me to leave her alone, she seemed happy.

"I should have come along," Amy said. "I don't know why I didn't."

"It's a hard thing to do, to leave them behind. I thought it was a hard thing to do."

"I should have come."

Even when we stopped talking I didn't feel like I could hang up. Amy was just waiting on the other end. Eventually she said, "What are you thinking right now?"

"About what?"

"You know what I mean."

So we lay there a little more. "You never mention it so I

don't know if you still think about it, but I've been thinking about it a lot," she said. "About the fact that Michael was . . . the same age as I was when my father died, whether maybe that had something do with what happened."

"I thought you were fourteen; he was twelve."

"Is that your reaction to what I just told you?"

After a minute, I said, "Did you talk about this with Dr. Pendleton?"

"What's that got to do with anything?"

"I'm just wondering if this is the kind of thing you talk about."

"Of course we talk about it."

"What does she think?"

"She thinks . . . that's not really how it works, you know that. We just talk, and she asks me questions. Why? Do you really care what she thinks? If she says yes, that's why you had an affair, does that mean . . ."

"It just seems like one of the stories people tell about themselves. Maybe it's true. I don't know. I don't know how we can tell the difference, if it is or not. I don't see that it changes anything."

"God, you're cold," she said.

"Okay."

But it still wasn't over—we lay there in bed, four hundred miles apart.

"I thought it might make you understand or be . . . more sympathetic to what I was going through, and why I did what I did."

"I've always been . . . being sympathetic to you has never been a problem for me."

"That's not what it feels like, over here."

"Well, I'm sorry about that."

"I'm going now," she said. "Goodbye," and hung up.

But even with the phone dead I couldn't sleep.

In grad school, when we lived together, I used to talk to Sam about Amy. You forget how up in the air all this stuff is at the beginning, the changing allegiances, the life decisions. I wanted to drop out, which Sam actually encouraged me to do, but he didn't think law school should be the next move; he wanted me to be a writer. I felt like, in grad school, all I encountered was a very narrow slice of America, basically made up of the people who cared about grades, which is. . . which is really not the most interesting thing to care about. He said law school would be even worse.

One of my ideas was to write a book about pickup basketball. I missed playing. For four years I sat on the bench at Pomona. Senior year I averaged maybe ten minutes of game time, and two or three points a night. That's the kind of player I was. But I liked hanging out with the guys, most of whom were better than me, which I compensated for by feeling smarter than they were, in ways that allowed me to appreciate more clearly how they were better. That seemed like a good emotional starting point for being a writer. My idea was to drive around America in a beat-up car and stop at various towns, big and small, and play pickup at some local court, famous or not, and write about the people I met there.

Sam, who went to Exeter and Princeton and then Harvard, thought it was a terrific idea. He said he was jealous of the access I had to this kind of world. We were twenty-five years old. These are the conversations we had.

While all this was going on, I had started communicating again with my girlfriend from Pomona, Jill McGurk, who was living in Las Vegas and working on the sports desk for the *Review-Journal*. Later she got involved in local politics.

We met freshman year, at an audition. By Thanksgiving, we had slept together, and for the rest of our four years never acted again. But we were a pretty solid couple, with a few standard infidelities and hiatuses. For some reason, the topic of staying together after graduation never came up seriously between us. I got into BU, and Jill wanted to stay closer to her mother, who lived in Holbrook, about a five-hour drive from Las Vegas. Close but not too close; she had a complicated relationship with her family. At Pomona I liked to think of myself as lower-middle class because my dad skipped out in high school, and after that we had a decent-sized house in a nice neighborhood in Trenton but not much money. If I wanted to I could say I was raised by a single mom. But my father worked in pharmaceuticals, he was definitely white-collar. Jill's mother had her when she was seventeen years old. Her parents ran the local Anglo-Mexican restaurant, Gringo's, just off Route 66, where Jill spent her summers working as a waitress, even after she made it to Pomona.

Her dad was her mom's high-school history teacher, who was married and got fired, and afterward moved to Tucson. She had a half brother who was eight years older and worked for the Sierra Club. But Jill was the first person on her mother's side of the family to go to college.

That she got into Pomona, which is a fairly ritzy school, was proof of the fact that Jill's an impressive and driven human being. At Holbrook High, she captained the volleyball team, which sucked, graduated salutatorian, and even got elected Homecoming Princess, which means she came second in that vote too. People liked her even though she was a high achiever. She kept up a good relationship with her dad, who used to see her three or four times a year, mostly to go camping, and often sent her books and newspaper or magazine articles he thought she might be interested in. She knew the *Spoon River Anthology* by heart. Part of what she liked about me is that I wanted to be a writer; I think she was disappointed when I opted for grad school. Maybe that was one of the reasons we split up. There was just a flatness in our relationship, where she had kind of realized I didn't have the guts to go all out for something I wanted, and I had realized about her . . . that this was how she saw me.

But there were other things going on too. Her mother, who was only forty, had rheumatoid arthritis and had taken over the restaurant, which she struggled to run on her own. Jill didn't want to get bogged down in all that. Holbrook is a pretty strange place, and she didn't want to end up there.

But she also wanted to be close enough that she could drive home on a Friday night and see what the situation was. Five hours in the car isn't anything to these people. Then she got the job in Las Vegas and it seemed totally normal for us to say goodbye, after three and a half years of sharing a bed. Move on with your life. Remember each other as college sweethearts before you grew up to be what you eventually became.

Except that, three years later, I was sick of grad school, and Jill wanted a break from the high-school sports desk. We started talking several nights a week on the phone. She even flew out once, at the end of summer, to visit me in Boston. Sam thought she was a knockout. Jill had put on a little weight but didn't care and used to carry herself like a waitress, who can attract attention and put guys off at the same time without hurting any feelings. About five-nine, red-blonde hair, she wore jeans and button-up shirts, so if she ever put on a dress you really noticed. We had a good time together, but I still felt she was holding something back. There was a guy in Vegas she had some kind of off-on commitment to, so even when she came to visit, she wouldn't go all the way. Her mom was Catholic, too, that was part of the story. But we made out like high school kids, which in its own way was even more intense. Then a few weeks later I went to a party at Ethan's place and met Amy.

Still, all through that year, I was talking to Jill on the phone, and talking to Brian Palmetto about moving to LA, and talking to Sam about the pickup book. And seeing Amy, and doing a little work for my LSATs, to see if maybe I could get into a decent law school and change my life in financially measurable ways.

These are the things I thought about when I couldn't sleep. Then, when I woke up, I didn't know where I was. I remembered feeling heartbroken about something and then realized it was Miri—she had gone.

Deborah and Sam were already having breakfast, I could hear them when I went to the bathroom. Their voices carried clearly up the stairwell.

"I didn't say that."

"What?"

"I didn't say what you said I said."

There were other kitchen noises, someone was emptying the dishwasher. Then he said, "He doesn't assume anything about you. He has other fish to fry."

"How long is he staying?"

"I think he's going home today."

"That's not the impression I got," Deborah said.

Then I took a leak and brushed my teeth, and afterward put on shorts and running shoes and went downstairs. Deborah was now alone in the kitchen.

"I'm making coffee," she said. "Do you want some?"

"I'm going for a run. Will you be here when I get back?"

"Probably not."

We looked at each other and I had a strong desire to say something meaningful to this young woman, maybe even to

84

explain myself, but what did she care. Even at breakfast she looked the way she looked getting off the plane, tired and put-together.

"Well, maybe I'll see you at lunch," I said and went past her into the hallway. "Which way is the park?" I called out.

"Left." And that was our last interaction.

It was maybe eighty degrees outside and ninety percent humidity, a real warm wet laundry morning. I started jogging up North Sheridan, past the mansions and the beautiful lawns and the telephone poles and real estate signs. Taking it easy, because I didn't want to set off any palpitations. You have to wiggle a little at the end, but I reached the park eventually. There are roads running through it, it's easy to get disoriented; I was looking for the river but couldn't find it. For some reason I had left my phone behind. Eventually I stopped and asked directions to North Sheridan, then I walked for a while and started running again. It was almost ten when I reached the house.

The door was locked and Sam's car was gone, so I sat on the steps between the pillars and waited. Feeling all right, with the sweat on me, and like, it's a summer morning and I'm not in any hurry. Like a young man.

About twenty minutes later, Sam pulled into the drive.

"I'm sorry," he said. "I was just giving her a ride into campus. She hates going back after any kind of a break."

"Does the department know?"

"About what?"

"About you and Deborah?"

"I don't know."

By this point we were in the house and Sam was making another pot of coffee. For a while he kept me company while I ate my breakfast, still sweating. "What are you going to do now?" he said.

"I guess go home."

"You want to have lunch first?"

"Sure. Where?"

So he suggested his club downtown, in case I wanted to see the city. "Have you got a jacket? If not, you can borrow one." So we talked about his club for a while. At one point he said, "To answer your previous question, you're supposed to declare these things. If you want to start a relationship with a grad student. Let the Chair know. And remove yourself from all official responsibilities. But I was never her supervisor in the first place. Anyway, it doesn't matter . . . there's nobody I have to pretend to be ashamed in front of." Which is what he said to me the day before. "Have you talked to Amy?" he asked suddenly.

"About what?"

"I thought you said you guys had a fight."

"I called her last night. But I don't know if we had a fight." I tried to explain myself. "For the past . . . I don't know, two or three years, she's been seeing a therapist, which means when you argue with Amy, it's like there's this other person in the room, who's a certified expert, and you have to argue with her, too. But we didn't really argue, we disagreed."

86

"About Miri."

Which wasn't what I meant, but I was glad to talk about something else.

"Yes. No. You have these ideas about your kids, which are probably just . . ."

"Projections?"

"It doesn't really matter if they are. Because if you have an idea about your kid, then that's a part of the kid, which she has to deal with whether it's wrong or right . . . so you have to be careful what you think about them. This is what I try to tell Amy. But she finds it hard not to have opinions about certain things."

"I'm not sure I know what you're talking about."

"That's okay," I said and looked at him, thinking, this old friend. At a certain stage of our lives. He gave me the same look back. But there was also a feeling like, something intimate was on the edge of the conversation, like, waiting to get in, which maybe in the past we might have let in, but the party was over now. Anyway, he had a squash date, I needed a shower. He left me a house key on the kitchen counter next to the sink and told me to meet him at one o'clock at the Duquesne Club, so I said sure. "We can pick this up then," he said. Then when he left he called something up the back stairs.

I was in my towel in the bathroom, with the water running, and couldn't hear him. "What?"

But he said it again, so I turned the water off and went down.

87

"Here's a jacket for you, in case you need it," and he hung it over one of the kitchen chairs.

"Fancy." It was an old Harris Tweed, a flea-market find.

"Well, it's something. It means they'll let you in."

"Thank you."

"Lunch may be more expensive than you had in mind, but it's on me."

"We can argue about that later," I said. Then he left and I went upstairs.

Coming out of the shower, I saw two missed calls on my phone, from Amy and Brian Palmetto. From an hour ago, when I was running in Highland Park. No message from Amy but Brian left a long voicemail. "Hey, Tom, can you give me a call? I need some legal advice. The Nuggets fired me yesterday but that's not what I'm talking about." There were background noises that made it hard for me to hear him. Somewhere in the room a printer was churning out pages. "I got a kid here, Todd Gimmell, who's been staying with me for a couple of days . . . he played for us last year, on a two-way contract. Anyway, he wants to bring a class-action lawsuit against the club. For systematic discrimination against white players. Very smart kid, real head on his shoulders. This may be what you've been looking for. I mean, the prima facie evidence is overwhelming. So call me. This is our chance to get some of our own back," Brian said.

I sat on the bed in my towel and listened to it again. What did he think we've been looking for? At least I didn't have to say anything, it was just a voice on a phone.

By this time it was almost eleven o'clock. I had a few hours to kill before lunch and told myself, enjoy the morning. For a while I walked through the empty rooms, imagining Sam's life. He had a lot of empty rooms. Why don't you read a book for a change . . . so I picked a book from the shelf and tried to read. *The Long Revolution*, by Raymond Williams, one of those old Pelican paperbacks, which I'd read in college for my Inventing Modernity seminar. But there are things you read in college that you can never read again. You don't have the attention span, you don't really care anymore. This isn't my life, I didn't want to sit around Sam's house all day, but I also didn't have anything else to do.

So go, get out, drive around.

All I had was a backpack; it didn't take long to pack. In the end I decided to leave his keys by the kitchen sink—I didn't plan on coming back after lunch.

At first I drove up North Sheridan toward the park, the same way I'd run, and thinking for some reason about Ethan Konchar. He doesn't really figure in my life these days but I'm going to talk about him anyway. Ethan was one of those guys that college friends gossip about when they meet up. After Göttingen he went to San Francisco and got involved in various tech start-ups. A couple of them made a lot of money. Real money but not like, philanthropy money, where you can spend the rest of your life playing with world problems. I would guess, thirty million dollars. Later, he used some of it to run for the California Senate, and after three terms of state politics got approached by the Democrats to go for the 4th Congressional District when Frank Riggs retired. Which he won, narrowly; he represented Napa Valley, where he also owned a fairly successful vineyard. After that he spent ten years in Washington, first as a congressman and then running a political advisory firm. I think that's what they call it.

Obama, before he left, appointed him US Ambassador to London.

But this is not why I thought about him. When he broke up with Amy, it was her first experience of being dumped by a guy who realized she wasn't ambitious enough for him. Or at least, who decided she wasn't part of his ambitions. This is something she was in the process of internalizing when we started going out. Who wants to do that? But it's also part of what attracted me to her, or made me sympathetic; at that time, I was in drop-out mode myself. First I wanted to be a professor, then I wanted to be a writer, but I ended up going to law school because . . . I thought, just live a nice life, where you can pay for nice things, which I wanted to do partly because of Amy. She gave me a sense for the first time of how nice a life you can buy, if you have the right tastes and know the right people.

This is more or less the life we lived.

At the time, though, I wondered what she saw in me. I wasn't Jewish, I wasn't at Harvard. I was just some guy . . . working on a dead-end PhD, who spent his weekends making money as a check-in agent at Logan. In other words, basically adrift, at the one period in her life where she was drifting, too. Since I had a car, we used to go for dates by driving out of Boston. The best thing about Boston is how easy it is to get out of it. Half an hour later, you're at Walden Pond. Thoreau in those days was one of my big influences and I tried to show off by taking all that stuff seriously. We walked around the water, we went antiquing in Concord, we drove out to Salem. I was like, her existentialist boyfriend, who questioned the point of everything, and she was the nice girl who brought me round, who pointed out, there are things worth living for.

My phone rang again and I pulled over to answer it, in case Miri was calling. By the time I parked and fished it out of my backpack, the ringing had stopped. It was Amy, and I suddenly remembered that I'd left Sam's jacket on the kitchen chair. So if I wanted to have lunch with him I needed to find another jacket.

I tapped on Maps and put in the Duquesne Club—about a twelve-minute drive if you took the highway. Then I typed in Denver Colorado. Twenty-one hours. I was pulled over on a kind of sidewalk, next to a rusty corrugated fence. Thick woodland climbed up the shoulders on either side. If you call Amy now the person you talk to will not be the person in your head, for whom you have these warm and simple feelings. It will be another person, who doesn't like you much these days, with whom you get into stupid arguments. Also, I didn't want to explain myself to her, what I was doing, at least until it was clearer to me. I got back on the road and followed it through the park until I hit a T-junction and saw the river on the other side, or guessed it was there, the mighty Allegheny, half-hidden by trees.

My phone said, go left. But I didn't really want to talk to Sam either. When we hit a bridge there were signs for Butler and Sharpsburg, so I crossed over the river and headed north.

One of my ideas was, maybe I could stay with my brother in South Bend. At least for a few days. And then work out what to do next.

My relationship with Eric is not totally straightforward. For one thing, he's six years younger, and when your dad moves out while you're in high school, and your kid brother is only eight at the time, that means in practice that you have different childhoods. Eric was very much a momma's boy, he pretty much cut off contact with Dad as soon as he was old enough to have a choice about it, and I don't think it cost him much. But it was harder for me to let go. This was one of our differences.

What I mean by momma's boy is . . . he was someone who didn't understand what it takes to get by in a world that isn't filled with people who love you. He thought all you have to do is be nice and nice things will happen. After college, he moved to LA and tried to become an actor. At Notre Dame, which actually has a terrific theater program, he was one of the standouts. Sometimes, when I want to annoy Amy, I tell her that's where Miri gets her talent from. But he had a hard time in LA. For one thing, he's good-looking, but it doesn't always show up on camera. His face is too small; his features seem pinched together. (He looks like our mother.) But honestly I don't know why people make it or don't in that world. Maybe it doesn't mean anything.

He was more successful in the LA theater scene. I saw him play Richard Rich in *A Man For All Seasons*; he has a good low-key English accent, which not everybody in the cast could pull off. But it's tough to make a living like that. Meanwhile, he tried to keep up a long-distance relationship with his college sweetheart, who stayed on to get her BSN and then landed a job at Memorial Hospital in South Bend. Terry actually grew up there; she was still living at home. So this was Eric's wild life as an actor in LA. Whenever he got the chance he kept flying back to Indiana to sleep in his girlfriend's parents' guest room.

Eventually he got sick of this life and married the girl and started working for an educational charity in South Bend, which brought acting classes into elementary schools. They had three kids, and then the marriage went sour, for reasons he never explained to me. But because they're Catholic she didn't want a divorce. So now he rents a two-bed apartment downtown and sees the girls on Wednesday night and every other weekend. (This is what my mother tells me, which is where I get most of my Eric-related information.) If I timed it right I could sleep in one of the bunkbeds for a couple of days.

By now I was on I-76 heading west, with about a quarter tank of gas. It was almost one o'clock and I hadn't eaten anything since a bowl of Great Grains at Sam's house after my run. Exit signs for Cleveland and Akron had started to appear.

Since I didn't have any reason for being in either, I turned off randomly and spent an hour driving through pretty suburban scenes—pine trees in the front yard, single story houses, churches, mailboxes on the curb—looking for somewhere to eat. Eventually of course I'd have to call Amy. It worried me also that she could track me on her phone, which might worry her, so I pulled over at a gas station and filled the tank and bought a Rand McNally Road Atlas of the United States. Then I powered off the phone.

This scared me a little. Maybe for the first time I realized what I was doing. But I also felt like, all right, kid, from here on out it's only you.

I guess downtown Akron has a skyline but I didn't get near it. This was strip-mall territory, where America makes it easy for you to park, and I stopped at a place called the Springfield Tavern. On the block next door there was a baseball school, whatever that means—a small brick warehouse offering private instruction. Across the street, I could see a tattoo parlor (the Ink Monkey), a workout shack (Strongman Gym), a liquor store, and a tire shop. A lot of one-room businesses. But there were also private homes in between, with gables and porches and well-mowed front yards.

The tavern was just a brown box, with most of the windows covered up; the sign outside said Monday Night Karaoke, Wed Bike Nite. But on Sunday afternoon I figured you'd have a lot of guys eating burgers and drinking beer and watching preseason football on TV. Which is more or less what I found, but the game behind the bar was a baseball game,

Indians/Tigers, except they aren't called the Indians anymore. The Cleveland Guardians, down five two in the fifth. So I sat at the bar and ordered a bourbon burger and a Heineken and watched the game, and just waited there, thinking, what the hell are you doing, but not unhappy, until the beer arrived.

I thought, you need some clothes. All I had in my backpack was last night's underwear and socks.

So I asked the guy two bar stools over where you could pick up some clothes around here, and he said, what kind of clothes. He was sitting on his own with a full pitcher of something golden, but then after a minute, a woman came out of the bathroom and sat down between us.

He said to her, "You all right?" and she said, "Not really."

"Do you want to go home?"

And she said, "Hair of the dog, right?"

"Maybe you should eat something."

"Maybe later."

"This gentleman here says he wants to go *clothes* shopping."

"What kind of clothes," she said.

"Just the necessaries," and she laughed. She had a heavy face and soft thinning light-brown hair falling across it. The guy looked older; he had a hearing aid in his ear and papery, reddish, well-shaved cheeks. I thought he might be her dad, which in fact he was.

We watched the game for a while, and eventually the woman said, "There's a Walmart about five minutes away. You just go down Krumroy and turn left. But I don't know why I'm telling you. Everybody just looks at their phone."

"I'm trying to live without my phone for a while."

"Noble ambition. Come on, Rosario," the guy said.

The batter blooped a single to right field and somebody scored—five three. There were two outs and men at the corners, and Ramirez was at the plate. We watched the pitch count go up, a strike, a couple of balls, another strike. Then Ramirez lined out to second and the inning was over. The show went to commercials; the sound was off, but it's funny how people stare at the screen anyway. Somebody was trying to clean a dog on their kitchen tiles.

I felt a little awkward sitting there, like I was in their living room. For some reason I said, "I just dropped my daughter off at college."

"That can hit you pretty hard."

"How would you know?" the woman asked.

"*You* went to college."

"For about a week. Then you had to come pick me up again." She looked at me with her chin in her hand. "I had a boyfriend situation back home." Then she said to her father, "That ended well."

"Where's she going?" he asked, and for a second I didn't know what he was talking about.

"Carnegie Mellon."

"Smart girl. You live around here? I guess not."

"Scarsdale. Westchester county."

"You're headed in the wrong direction," he said.

Then the food arrived and it seemed easier not to talk. But we stayed till the end of the game. Cleveland actually took the lead in the 8th on a three-run homer by Josh Naylor and then hung on to win, with Sam Hentges on the mound. "You guys big Guardians fans?" I said at one point, just to say something.

"Please," she said. "In this place we can still call them what they are."

After the game, she finished the pitcher and slowly stood up; she put a hand on her father and then a hand on me. "If you're not doing anything later," she said, "we're having a cookout at my dad's place about seven o'clock."

"Diane," her father said.

"What, I'm just being friendly."

"I guess you guys are making a day of it."

"Well, it's my birthday, isn't it. I got the whole rest of my life for being depressed."

"Diane," her father said again.

"It doesn't matter. People don't listen to me anyway." But she told me the address on Beach Drive Extension. "He's got a real nice setup," she said. "Right on the water."

"He doesn't want to have dinner with us."

"Who knows what he wants to do," she said and put her hand on my cheek. She had nice soft hands. "I want to see those new clothes." Then they left and it was three o'clock in the afternoon and I was sitting in the dark bar, staring at the TV.

Back in the car, a few minutes later, I thought, this is stupid, and switched on my phone. Walmart really was a five-minute drive away, I could have followed her directions. But there was another missed call from Amy. She said, I just want to know when you're getting home . . . what the dinner plan is. I listened to her in .the Walmart parking lot, which is big enough for an airport. Then I sat in the car for a while. Eventually I called Eric and left a message. Listen, I said, I might be passing by your neck of the woods tomorrow and wondered if you could put me up. Just for a night or two. It'd be good to see you, been too long. Etc. etc. Then I turned off the phone again and got out of the car.

If you ever want to feel your place in the scales of the universe, go into a Walmart Supercenter. It's a universe that offers a lot of almost identical and not very attractive choices. All I had with me was running shoes and shorts, and the Levi's and old high-top Converse All-Stars I was walking around in. For about an hour I just drifted under the high hangar roof in a state of bewilderment. But I picked up a few white T-shirts, a pack of Hanes briefs, and some socks. The only thing that cost more than twenty bucks was a plain green Wrangler collared shirt, which cost $24.99, in case the nights got cold. I also bought another bag of Entenmann's Pop'ettes, a party-size Fritos Original, and a twelve-pack of Dr. Pepper for the drive, to keep me awake on the road.

Then I figured, you should get something for Eric's kids, but I didn't really know these girls at all. The last time I saw them was three years ago, when our mother had knee-replacement surgery and we took turns visiting and helping out. It was the summer, there was a few days' overlap, and

Eric brought the girls to cheer her up. The youngest was Sally, I had a decent relationship with her. She let me teach her how to use a baseball glove, which means catching in your off hand and takes getting used to. The middle kid was probably on the spectrum but hadn't been diagnosed—her mother was against all that. Anyway, she didn't interact with people she didn't know, which included me. The oldest, Daryl, was twelve and looked seventeen and flirted with everybody, men and women; I tried to give her some room. But all of this information was out of date.

In the end, I bought a bagful of Reese's, Hershey's, Kit Kats and M&Ms, assorted chocolate crap, and a 175g Discraft Frisbee, since every child should grow up with the real thing. Anyway, this was the phrase running through my head at the checkout counter, when I imagined seeing Eric and handing over the loot. Who knows if you say it or not. I also bought a Wilson Street Shot Outdoor basketball, just for . . . something to do, which I didn't have a lot of. I asked the checkout clerk if there was anywhere in the neighborhood to shoot hoops.

"Is this a neighborhood?" he said. He had a Shaggy Rogers haircut and one of those half-inch disk earrings in his left earlobe, mostly hidden by hair.

"You know what I mean."

"Not really. You could try East Liberty Park, but I don't know if they have a court."

"How far is that?"

"About five minutes."

So an hour later and a hundred bucks poorer, I walked out again into the late summer Akron afternoon.

To get there you go under the interstate, about sixty yards of highway crossing at an angle over your head. The other side is more strip-mall-land. But then you turn again and come off the main road, and the suburbs seem almost rural, a few houses, a lot of open ground, and East Liberty Park.

The park is big enough it took me a while to find the courts, but I didn't mind driving around. The skies had cleared, it was almost six o'clock and still eighty-five degrees outside according to my dashboard thermometer. Just that point in the evening when a kid starts thinking, why do I have to go home. When I was a teenager, in what turned out to be the last year of my parents' marriage, I used to come back after school and head straight out again to Cadwalader Park, across the canal. Since I didn't have any friends (we had just moved to Trenton), I took a basketball. If there were kids around, I could play with them; if not, I worked on my jump shot.

There were a couple of courts, side by side, and then a long row of tennis courts across a chain-link fence, most of them empty. A black guy, maybe thirty years old, in a sort of blue medical shirt, was shooting around on one of the hoops, so I set up on the other end and did the same. Sometimes, chasing down a miss, I stopped to watch what he was working on— midrange turnarounds, after a little shimmy, over and over again. Most of them went in. Eventually he looked back at me and said, "Hey."

"What's up?"

"You want to play one-on-one?"

"Sure," I said.

I was still wearing jeans and my old Chuck Connors, but what the hell. I'm fifty-five years old, it doesn't matter if you lose. But of course it still matters. There's always a moment before you start when you have no idea if you're even in the other guy's league. His name was Frank, he worked at the Cleveland Clinic, this was just a stop-off on his way home. To unwind, so he didn't bring his work back with him. I said I just dropped my daughter at college and was driving out to South Bend to see my brother. Frank said he had a little girl, eight years old, but she lived with her mother. I was young and stupid, he said. Now I'm just stupid. He had one of those fifties-style close-shaved moustaches, short hair, strong forearms; maybe he was five-ten, five-eleven, a few inches shorter than me.

"Ones and twos?" I said. "First to eleven, win by two. You make it you take it."

"Fine by me."

We used his ball. He let me take it out and set up three or four feet away, with his hands on his knees, waiting for me to do something. So I shot; it went in. He gave it back to me and I shot again. Four nothing.

"So it's like that," he said and started D-ing me up.

It was a friendly game, but he played hard; he was faster than me, and stronger, but he liked to cheat on defense. If you waited for him to reach, you could get by him, you just had to push the ball ahead and chase it down. Also, I was long enough to bother his release; those midrange turnarounds weren't falling anymore. I won the first game eleven four, but in the second he got a little angry, at himself as much as anything, and backed me down, pounding the ball and shoving his butt against me, pushing me under the basket. My legs were tired, I started shooting flat and short. At five up, I said, "Give me a minute." I was breathing heavy, one of my shoe laces was undone. I bent over to tie it up and a noise like a howitzer went off in my ears, my eyes darkened, and I had to sit down on the hard court by the free-throw line.

"You okay," he said, standing over me.

"Just give me a minute." I could see again.

"I'll bet that's not the first time that happened."

"No." I reached out a hand, and he pulled me up.

"Listen," he said. "Why don't I drive you over to the clinic and get you checked out. If I take you in, you won't have to wait."

"I'm all right. It usually passes pretty quick."

"You sure?"

"Let's finish the game."

"No way," he said, but in the end we played on. He went easy on me, I hit a couple of threes. Afterward, I said, "Do you mind if I take a picture? I'm writing a book about pickup basketball in America."

"Are you a writer?"

"I used to want to be."

He stood with the ball in his hands, under the basket, and had a kind of attractive personal vanity, which made him stand at attention for the camera. He had very good posture. Then he took a picture of me, and I took a few more, of the park and the tennis courts, and the chain-link fence. He watched me and said, "I played in high school but was mostly just goofing around. You can tell when someone used to be serious. Now I'm thirty-three years old and trying to work on my game, but it's too late."

For some reason, he was in confidential mode. We walked to our cars together. He said, "You got any other symptoms?"

"Sudden fatigue. Headrushes, if I get up too quick, or bend down. Well, you saw."

"Any chest pain? Any trouble breathing?"

"No. A little arrhythmia. In the morning I wake up, my face is like a water balloon."

"You need to get that checked out," he said. "God gives you symptoms for a reason."

He drove a Mazda Miata, with a low front seat, so he had to duck his head to get in. There was sweat on the back of his blue shirt, in a Rorschach pattern under his shoulder blades. When he was gone, I thought, well, now what? So I sat in the car and called Amy.

She answered at the first ring. "Tom, Tom. Where are you? You sound out of breath."

"I've been playing pickup."

"Where are you? Are you all right?"

"I'm fine."

"Did it happen again?"

"What?"

"The thing that happens sometimes, when you overdo it."

"I didn't overdo it, I'm fine."

"Where are you? When are you coming home?"

"I'm in Akron," I said.

"I don't understand."

"I got a call from Brian Palmetto, who needs some legal help. He just got fired."

"So what does that mean?"

"I thought I might drive out there, since I'm in the car."

"I don't know what that means."

"Well, I wanted to let you know."

We sat there for a minute in silence and I wondered where she was. I had dialed the home number, and there was a handset in the kitchen by the cereal shelf.

"What kind of legal help?"

"There's a class-action suit, I don't really know the details. That's what I want to talk to him about."

"What about your teaching?"

After a moment, I said, "I'm on leave this term."

"Since when?"

"I thought you knew."

"I didn't know. Did something happen?"

"We haven't been communicating very much."

"Whose fault is that?"

"Mostly mine. I'm just . . . a little adrift right now. I can't seem to get a grip on anything."

And then she said, which I didn't think she would, "Me neither."

"I just need a few days to get my head on straight."

"But I don't understand why you're in Akron. I don't understand."

"I thought I might see my brother. On the way. That's where I'm headed tomorrow night."

"Oh," she said, and then, out of habit, "Say hi from me."

"I will. It's nice to talk to you. Amy?"

"What?"

"I need to get away from the phone for a few days, too. Before I do I'll call Michael as well. I'll let Miri know."

"What happens next?"

"I don't know. I'll call you," and she said, "Don't expect me to be waiting by the phone."

Afterward, I drove around for a while in no particular direction. Just seeing the sights. I even stopped by the house on Beach Drive Extension. It's true, you could see water between the trees. A wide curbless street, telephone poles sticking out of the front yards; nice modest houses, brick ranch houses with front porches, a few of them had new siding. I heard her voice again, I got the whole rest of my life for being depressed. It was almost seven o'clock and a boombox or whatever they're called these days blasted "Heads Carolina" from the backyard. I pulled over for a minute. The driveway had a long line of cars backed up on the loose gravel.

Somebody honked getting out, and I drove on.

The road dead-ended in a footpath running between the front yards; eventually in the distance it became a dirt trail. So I turned around and passed the house again, thinking of a conversation I had with Michael when he was seven or eight years old. His friends had played a trick on him in school—I don't remember the trick, some practical joke. One of them was Mike Camaro, also known as Other Mike, his best friend. So Michael said to him, "In that case you're not invited to my birthday party." Maybe he was seven going on eight, his birthday party was coming up. The problem was, if he said something he stuck to it; I kept trying to talk him down. We knew Other Mike's parents, I didn't want the whole thing to blow up into some childhood scar. So I said to Michael, "Have you never played any practical jokes on Other Mike?"

He was lying in bed and I was sitting next to him, on the little Robin Day chair we gave him for laying out his clothes. Michael didn't like people sitting on his bed, even as a seven-year-old.

"Of course not."

"If you're going to learn how to forgive people you have to be willing to put yourself in the wrong sometimes."

"I don't want to put myself in the wrong."

"That can be a little lonely."

I took a right onto Beach Drive, back the way I had come; the boombox music faded away. It was just another suburban street where I had no reason to be. What I needed was to find something to eat and somewhere to sleep that night. Also, I had to call Eric again. About ten minutes later I saw a sign for the airport and turned onto 77, heading north, because I figured that's where most of the hotels would be, off the highway.

When the kids were small we took them on a road trip through the southwest, New Mexico, Arizona, Utah, all the big national parks. Anyway, the thing they liked most was the Comfort Inn outside Carlsbad Caverns. It had a swimming pool that stayed open until ten o'clock, protected from the traffic noise by a stand of pine trees. There were kids in the pool until closing, and Michael watched them playing, using Miri as a comfort blanket, someone he had to look out for—she had just learned to swim. In the morning, the breakfast bar had a waffle maker. So Michael and Miri made their own waffles. Afterward this place became the family standard against which all other human experiences were measured. Did you sleep all right? I slept okay, but it wasn't like Comfort Inn. How was breakfast? Etc.

There was a Comfort Inn & Suites, next to a TGI Friday's, but you actually couldn't get there from the highway. I had to take the next exit and noodle around past various car dealerships and fast-food outlets before I found it. I don't even know if the chains are related, but it didn't matter. I checked in. Then the long night awaited: lonely dinner at Friday's, calling Eric, calling Michael and leaving a message, calling Brian Palmetto, watching TV in bed, trying to sleep.

I tried to write a little, at about two in the morning. I figured I should write up my game with Frank at East Liberty Park if

I was going to do a book about pickup basketball . . . but I didn't have anything to write with, except the hotel stationary. And nothing came anyway. The pad was about as big as my hand, I stared at it for five minutes trying to come up with a good first line. "People reveal themselves on the basketball court . . ." That obviously wasn't it. "They don't just come to play, they come to talk." Which is just untrue. It was like grad school again, when I tried to churn out my dissertation on Updike and realized, I don't want to write about other people's experiences or ideas of the world, I want to have my own; but I didn't really want to do that either. I just wanted to sit around and read books for the rest of my life.

There's an old Paul Simon line, "I don't expect to sleep through the night," which I think about sometimes in the small hours. Sometimes I carry on conversations in my head, trying to explain myself or re-narrate certain events. That night, after turning out the light, I lay in bed and talked to Amy about our first apartment in New York. I started out clerking for Judge Mattieson at the Second Circuit Court of Appeals. After that I spent two years at Draxell and Schmidt just to pay off my law school debts. Amy got a job at Brearley. A lot of these high-end private schools have a habit of hiring their own. People go to them as privileged kids and then come back to teach there as less privileged adults, making thirty thousand dollars a year and living in studio apartments not much bigger than their old bedrooms.

Actually, we got a decent deal on a one-bed on E. 83rd, just off Second Avenue and four blocks from the school.

Amy taught history and ran the French Club. She had lived in Paris for two years as a girl; her French was practically native. In fact, when I listened to her talk it was a gentle reminder of what her personality used to be like, before being slowly eroded by long association with me. She sounded like a Naftali again, with a little gloss of confidence and manners; unreachable to me, but maybe that was just because I couldn't understand what she was saying. I did AP Spanish in high school.

French Club was mostly a lunchtime thing. They had a special table in the cafeteria, where Amy ate with her students once a week. Sometimes she brought in dishes she made at home or baguettes and brioche from Eli's on Third Avenue. But she also arranged after-school trips to the Cloisters Museum or to watch a movie at FIAF, the French Institute Alliance Française. There were only about six or seven girls who came along, but they obviously adored her, and who wouldn't. She looked like an old *Vogue* fashion-plate, in her long yellow Ralph Lauren overcoat; and unlike some of the younger teachers, who tried to act like high-school kids themselves, she treated her students like colleagues, politely and formally flirtatious, in the French style. Amy liked schoolgirl admiration. She dealt with it pretty well, most of the time.

One of the kids was a girl named Bianca Gertz, whose dad was chief executive of HBO. This meant that when he had an affair it showed up in the pages of the *Post*. I mention this only to give an idea of what Bianca was going through, to explain her behavior. But she developed a real fixation on Amy, which Amy found flattering at first and finally didn't know how to respond to. There were a lot of gifts in the early days, some of them inappropriately expensive. She came home one day with a charm bracelet from Harry Winston and I remember saying to her, you have to give that back. She said, how can I give it back, it will just upset her. Given what she's going through. And I said, well, you have to. Which she did in the end, setting off a whole chain of reactions and interactions, but maybe they would have happened anyway.

Bianca started calling us at home; I don't know how she got the number. Leaving messages or hanging up. Once I actually talked to her. Hi, may I please speak to Miss Naftali? A shy, reasonable New York voice. I'm sorry, she's not in right now, can I take a message. No, that's all right. Another girl in French Club said to Amy, you know she hangs around outside your building. How does she know, I said to Amy, and Amy said, I have no idea what goes on in their lives. On Friday nights we used to eat at Totonno's Pizzeria, the uptown branch. It had a wide window onto Second Avenue. Amy liked the vodka penne; anyway, a lot of her students used to pass by on the sidewalk. These were rich New York kids whose parents gave them a credit card for dinner. They roamed the streets.

We stopped going because Amy thought she saw Bianca walking past, not once but over and over, looking at us through the window each time. Apparently she was under the impression that Amy was stuck in some kind of coercive relationship, that I was the one who made her give back the bracelet (which was true), because I didn't want her to experience outside friendships. Bianca wrote her a long letter, in which she basically said, Look, I know you're asking for help, and I want you to know, I can be the person who helps you. The letter was waiting for us on the doorstep of our apartment—she must have come up the elevator and left it outside. Who knows how long she waited there. Amy wanted to throw the letter away. It made her unhappy, like it was radioactive, and any contact with these teenage-girl feelings might contaminate you. Her memories of her own unhappy teenage years after her father died were still too fresh. But I made her keep it, because I could see where this was heading.

She told her head of department, who wasn't at all surprised. Bianca's nickname in the staff lounge was the Utility Monster. She's a bright kid, she seems like a nice kid going through hard times, and after a while you realize, she's soaking up all of your attention. So Amy stopped running French Club. One of the French teachers took it over, and at the end of the semester it quietly disbanded. Since Bianca wasn't in any of her classes, that seemed the simplest solution. But she started showing up in the history office anyway. Always with some legitimate problem, an essay she wanted to go over. If Amy was around, she stopped by her desk afterward. How are you, Miss Naftali? Everyone says, French Club isn't the same . . .

Once, she chased her into the faculty bathroom. Amy had her period; she sat in the stall, and Bianca took the stall next door.

"I just want to talk to you, I know what you're going through. Believe me, that's one of the things I learned from my mother after all this. It's hard to walk out of an unhappy situation."

Amy said, "I can't talk to you anymore. You have to leave me alone."

A few days later, Bianca took her mother's bottle of Temazepam to school. She swallowed most of it at lunch, made it to class (Calculus), and put her head on the desk. When the teacher told someone to wake her up, they couldn't. But the ambulance came pretty quickly; Bianca knew what she was doing.

Afterward, the whole story came out, and the father threatened to sue the school. Amy spent hours with the lawyers, it was very upsetting. On one of their French Club outings, she took them to a screening of *Jules et Jim* at Film Forum. Five of them went, Amy, Bianca and three other girls. The movie ended around half past eight. One of the girls lived in the West Village and walked home. But all the rest lived on the Upper East Side. It was February and about twenty-five degrees outside. Amy decided to take a cab. Bianca was the last girl she dropped off, at her mother's apartment on 82nd and Park.

Bianca claimed that in the few blocks between 77th and Third, where they dropped one of the other girls, and her mother's place, Amy confessed her feelings. She said she can't stop thinking about me, but she's stuck in a relationship she doesn't know how to get out of, which is why she hasn't done anything yet. Not to mention that she's a teacher at my school . . . but she isn't going to be a teacher much longer. She wants to quit and do something else; she's very unhappy. Amy, of course, denied saying anything along these lines. Maybe I told her, teaching is hard, especially at the beginning, because Bianca said she wanted to be a teacher like me, at the place where she went to school, she didn't ever want to grow up . . . and that's what it must be like, teaching at your old school. We had a whole conversation about *that*, and I tried to say, coming back can be a little complicated emotionally, but that's all. I certainly didn't talk about my relationship or say anything about my *feelings*. Maybe I said that I worried about her sometimes, maybe I said something like that. But this is a girl who lives in a TV-show version of her own life, where she thinks the camera is always on her.

She showed the lawyers Bianca's letter, which was written a few weeks after the Film Forum trip and didn't mention anything about their cab ride uptown. Eventually the whole thing blew over, but it made the rest of the semester deeply unpleasant for Amy. She never felt confident that her colleagues believed her version of events, even though they knew Bianca was a piece of work. I told her, she should countersue the school for putting her in this position, after she had tried repeatedly to warn her head of department about Bianca's behavior. But she thought, if I do that, there's no way I can go back . . . and like I said, the whole thing blew over. The dad had money problems on top of everything else, he didn't need more legal fees. And Bianca, when she got out of the hospital, transferred to Riverdale Country.

But I think it's part of why, when Amy became pregnant with Michael that summer, she decided to quit. She was five months pregnant when we got married, a November wedding; we took our honeymoon in Cape Cod. And when we came home afterward she started looking for a house to buy in Westchester; she didn't want to raise a kid in the city. By that point I was already teaching at Fordham.

This is what I talked to her about as I lay in the Comfort Inn, this is what I tried to get straight in my head. Because when Bianca accused Amy of confessing her feelings in that cab, it put me in a tricky position. My main duty, as the loving boyfriend, was obviously to show complete faith in Amy's version of events. So that's what I did. But at the same time I felt uncomfortable totally ignoring the possibility that Amy was subconsciously trying to express some doubts about our relationship. Can your subconscious express itself through the self-absorption of a neurotic teenage girl? I don't know, but it wasn't a picnic for me either. In the long years afterward, it did occur to me sometimes that maybe Bianca had responded to *something*. That Amy even in those early days felt like she was giving ground to me.

I thought, if you turn on the TV it might help you fall asleep. You can watch *SportsCenter* on a loop.

Sometimes she complained, you don't need me. You don't need me like I need you. And I'd say, this is your world, the world we are living in, which I work hard to pay for, is your world not mine . . . but that's not really what she meant. She has a personality that is based on being generous, cherished, and depended on. Yet she ended up in an adult life where once the kids reached a certain age she had more hours in the day than she knew what to do with. The kids need you and then they withdraw their need, and you have to put up with it. So you become someone who is . . . unlike yourself, but how do you say this to a person you love. At three in the morning in a hotel bed.

It's about a five-hour drive from Akron to South Bend. Things get a little tricky on the outskirts of Cleveland, but after that you just stick to I-80. I stopped for gas and a Subway sandwich and reached my brother's apartment around two in the afternoon. He lived in an old hotel, which had been dolled up and turned into residential units. This was part of a compromise with his wife, who didn't like the thought of their kids living downtown (in South Bend! That hub of degenerate America), so he picked a doorman building to calm her down. But it meant he could only afford a two-bedroom; the girls had to sleep in one room. I had never been there before.

I don't see my brother often but whenever I'm about to . . . I feel this onrush of eagerness. All day it came in waves, as the miles strung out behind me. The highway takes you north of the city, and I turned off and drove past Notre Dame, then nosed along, following my phone and staring out of the window at every stoplight. South Bend is pretty wide open. The river is like another blue highway between roads. There are public gardens on street corners and low-rise banks and apartment buildings. It's funny to think, we grew up in the same house, but this is where he made his life.

The Hoffman is opposite a Burger King, where I left the car. Later I had to move it underground—his apartment comes with visitor parking.

Eric's working day is unpredictable. Sometimes he's in the office, but he also spends a lot of time visiting schools, not just in South Bend but across St. Joseph county. When I spoke to him on the phone, he promised to leave a key at the reception desk. It took him a while, but the doorman eventually found it and I let myself into Eric's empty home, which was on the sixth floor and had a view of the river from the kitchenette. But the whole place felt like a hotel, the carpeting, the furniture, the pillar holding up the living room, the windows that you couldn't open. At least the girls' room had toys on the floor and pictures on the wall—kid pictures in crayon and watercolor, stuck on with Blu-Tack. What was nice about the apartment is that you got the feeling he didn't care what it looked like to other adults, but that was also a little depressing.

I left my backpack on the floor and lay down for a minute in one of the bottom bunks. When I woke up Eric was leaning over me. The curtains were closed; it was still sunny outside, and the glow of the afternoon came through in dusty lines.

"I didn't know if I should wake you. It's after five."

"Hey." Then I said, "That's all right. I didn't sleep much last night. It's nice to see you."

Eric is six years younger than me, the same age gap as Michael and Miri. Whether you want to or not you end up reproducing the structure of your childhood. In Eric's case that meant he didn't really remember our father, I mean, as somebody who lived with us. The guy we spent two weeks in the summer with, at his house in Orange County, where he had another two kids, much younger, a new wife, and basically didn't want us around . . . that guy Eric knew well. But the other guy, on his first marriage, where Dad still thought, maybe I can live a life where I haven't made any unforgivable mistakes, where whatever we're going through is just the normal headache . . . he didn't remember.

When Dad left, Eric started sleeping in Mom's bed. Because he kept waking up with nightmares, she said, but really because she didn't want to sleep alone. This was tricky, because Eric still wet the bed. Even at seven years old; he had a bladder problem, and eventually my parents bought rubber sheets for him, so Mom didn't keep having to wash his bedclothes. But when he started sleeping with her, the same thing happened. I was old enough to help with the household chores, which included laundry chores. So sometimes I had to deal with their wet sheets. Every night she put him to sleep in his bed, and then, when she went up a few hours later, carried him over to her room. They had a relationship from which I was basically excluded, not that I really wanted any part of it. Eric had to absorb a lot of her craziness and unspent love.

The truth about Dad was, he didn't like small kids. He just didn't like them, which made it ironic that when he started an affair with Lisa, who was significantly younger and worked for Jannsen's office in LA, he eventually moved in with her and had two more kids. But he didn't mind teenagers, and that's what I was when he left. He taught me how to play cards, not just basic poker, but old-school games like casino and bridge. He had a funny way of laying down a winning card, where he didn't say anything, but just set it down a little heavy, so you noticed. He could shuffle a deck midair, which I spent hours practicing. Sometimes, on Saturday afternoons, he took Eric and me to Phillies games, but since Eric got carsick and generally made himself a pain in the neck, eventually he just took me. When he left it was harder for me to say, the guy's a jerk. Not that this was Eric's point of view, but there wasn't a big gap in his life after Dad walked out, which there was in mine.

All of this probably sounds like I resented my kid brother, which wasn't the case. I felt sorry for him and guilty about him. He was one of those kids who always gets what he wants and isn't very happy about it. For one thing, he was a very fat kid, until he hit puberty. I mean, fat enough that it was an impediment to certain activities. If I tried to talk to Mom about it, she just got stressed out—it was one more thing going wrong in her life. And she couldn't say no to him anyway, if he wanted soda for dinner or another bowl of mint chocolate chip. Part of why I went to Pomona was to get the hell out of New Jersey; also, maybe, because I thought I might see more of my dad. But that didn't really happen. Even though it's less than an hour's drive from Newport Beach, maybe I saw him five or six times in the whole four years. But I didn't know that when I went.

I felt bad about Eric, though, I really did. Leaving him alone with our mother, in that condition.

But he actually turned himself around. He lost a *lot* of weight. When I flew home the summer after freshman year, I almost didn't recognise him. He used adolescence as a chance to make certain decisions about himself, and who he wanted to become. So, no to all the cookies and Cokes, which my mother found hard to take—it was like a rejection of her love. He never liked sports but started jogging in the mornings and lifting weights after school. Even as a fat kid he had a kind of social confidence, he didn't mind attracting attention, which he found other ways of putting to good use. At some point I came home to a world where my dumb kid brother was the star of the school play and reading Walker Percy on the pot, so you couldn't get him out of the bathroom.

All of this came at a price, and not just for Mom. Somehow he didn't seem comfortable with this new identity in front of me. For example, he made Mom join a church, St. Hedwig's on Brunswick Avenue, just to get her out of the house, he said, so she could meet new people. But I think he also liked the idea of having a mission and a community, neither of which I've ever been a big fan of. So on Sunday mornings over the holidays I had to decide, do I go along or not. Eric made it pretty clear, I don't expect you to follow this new direction our lives have taken . . . which was both reasonable of him, but also like, leave us alone. So I left them alone. On the whole I was grateful he'd found a way to turn his unhappy energy outward, even if it meant I didn't get to play big brother. That's fine, that's okay; I mean, for eight months a year he was on his own. He couldn't rely on his big brother very much.

But still, every time I was about to see him, I felt this rush of childish eagerness clutching my heart, which was replaced, when I did see him, with something more complicated. A feeling like, we both have to protect ourselves against this level of intimacy.

He wanted to know how long I planned to stay, if I could stick around and see the girls, who came after school every Wednesday. But I told him, "I'm leaving tomorrow. I have to get to Denver."

"For what?"

"To see Brian Palmetto. But that's a longer conversation; it can wait."

I sat in his living room area on one of the low couches. He made me a cup of Celestial Seasonings. "What do you want to do?" he asked.

He took off his shoes in the house and stood on the thick carpet in his socks. Because of all those years of acting, he had good physical balance; he moved like an athlete. He also looked too skinny, if you asked me.

"I don't know, show me your life."

"What does that mean?"

"We can drive around, I wouldn't mind seeing the city."

"You've been driving all day."

"Well, you can drive."

So, that's what we did, but first I had to move my car from the Burger King into one of the Hoffman's visitor parking spots. So we got in my car then we got in his car. Eric drove an old Camry. It was basically his office, he spent a lot of time on the road. There were papers on the passenger seat, which he told me to throw in the back. "You see how I live," he said. But it pleased him, I think, to sit behind the wheel; it made the power relationship a bit easier.

We drove across the river to the girls' school, which took up several blocks behind a spear-topped iron fence. "That's where all my money goes," he said. You couldn't see much. There were trees in the way, and wide lawns, and vague collegiate-looking buildings in the distance. We parked for a minute on the other side of the street, in front of somebody's house. It was six o'clock. People were coming home after a workday, and we watched a couple of cars pull out of the long school driveway.

"But the girls are happy," he said. "At least at school."

"Is it a Catholic school?"

121

"More or less. Officially non-denominational. It's where Terry went. They're basically having her childhood . . . without the father." He laughed; he had a sweet, unhappy laugh. Eric unlike me had lost most of his hair and cut what was left pretty short, so he looked like a monk or a long-distance runner. To me he still looked like a kid, boyish and somewhat intense, but I realized that if I met him now I'd think, a middle-aged man.

"You want to see the house?"

"Sure. Won't that be a little weird?"

"We can just drive by."

"Maybe you could call and say their uncle's in town."

"I've learned it's better if you stick to the script."

Terry and the kids lived in Granger, about twenty minutes away by the Michigan border. But first he took me past her parents' place, which isn't the house she grew up in but where they moved after retiring. There was a cul-de-sac, with a circular drive at the end, around a patch of green lawn with a flagpole sticking out of it and an American flag flapping around on the pole. "Can you believe it?" Eric said. "You couldn't make it up. Thirty years ago, none of this was here, this wasn't even a place."

"What are they like?"

"Who? Terry's parents? I don't know. I can't describe them and sound like a sane person. We go to the same church."

"I didn't know you went to church anymore."

"Sometimes I take the girls." He was circling the flagpole.

Eventually he said, "They still introduce me to people as their son-in-law."

There were no other cars, the streets were wide and curbless. Most of the houses had extensive lawns, and sometimes at the end of a block there was open grassland, dotted with trees, so you couldn't always tell where one yard began and another ended. "That's it," Eric said, slowing down. "With the Honda in the driveway." In fact, all you could see of their house was the gray metal door of the garage.

We turned a corner but the rest of it was screened by trees. I had a slightly creepy feeling of déjà vu, like I was cruising around looking for Diane's party.

"I can't remember how long you lived there."

"Three years. First we had an apartment in Edgewater. Then we moved out here. I actually have a job offer in Chicago, but if I take it I'll never see the girls. Except maybe like Dad, for two weeks in the summer. I don't know. We can park and get out, nobody will see us."

He pulled over by the side of the road but we just sat there, under the trees. Eric turned off the engine.

"I may have walked out on Amy," I said.

"You may?"

"About ten years ago she had an affair with a guy from . . . our synagogue. I told myself, when Miri leaves home, then I can go too."

"You waited ten years?"

"It may have been more like twelve."

"Now you're just showing off."

One of the lights in the house came on, a downstairs window; dusk was setting in. Eric said, "That's the bathroom light."

"I forgot to give it to you, but I bought a few things for the kids."

"That's nice."

"Mostly candy, but I got them a Frisbee too. In case they didn't have one already. I don't know."

"That's nice." Then he said, "Terry always drives them to her parents' house. It's a ten-minute walk but she always takes the car. She won't even let the girls bike over there."

"Why not?"

"Traffic," he said. We sat in the dark car by the side of an empty street. "She lives in a world of fear. I couldn't take it anymore."

"You've done this before."

"The apartment isn't really a place I want to be in the evening if the girls aren't there. So I drive around."

"Listen," I said. "I need to cut loose a little. Is there somewhere we can get a beer?"

So that's what we did. He turned on the engine and we drove back into Edgewater, his old neighborhood. Nothing seemed very far away in South Bend, it's a shrinking city. We went to a place called Kelly's Pub; it was easy to park. Just a small windowless building on the corner of a large lot. I said to Eric as we walked in, "Can you eat here?" and he said, "You can eat." There was a pool table at the back, a couple were playing pool. But other than that it was fairly empty, it was Monday night. Just some people at the bar, which curved around the shelf with all the drinks—guys in trucker hats and women in shorts.

"I come here because Terry never would," Eric said. "They had a big shooting outside a few years ago."

"Is this where you take all your dates?"

We sat down near the pool table; a waitress came over. I ordered a French dip sandwich and an IPA with a stupid name. Eric went for the fish basket. We had a couple of pints before the food arrived. One of the things I forgot about my brother is that he giggles when he drinks, he gets happy pretty fast, until it turns into something else. We watched the people playing pool, the girl was better than the guy. He wore a Foegley Landscape short-sleeved collared shirt and looked about twenty-five. She was older, late thirties, early forties, on the heavy side but well made-up, with straight, dyed-black hair and bright red lipstick. A little Gothy, but like, now she had a job.

Maybe they weren't a couple but he kept trying to flirt with her. He said, "Play me again. I gotcha this time, I'm just screwing around. Oh come on." He kept putting quarters on the table.

"Terry says I have anger issues, but I think what I need to deal with is the stuff that makes me angry, that's what I need to deal with." Everything seemed funny to Eric. "I don't know, I'm working on regulating my moods. Regulating my *moods*." He repeated himself, too.

"Tell me about this job in Chicago."

"The company I work for has headquarters in Evanston. It's a step up the ladder, but it means not going into schools anymore. It's a lot more money."

"That's great, that's wonderful."

"I don't know. I need to do something different. But it's not like, back in college, I dreamed of working for an *educational charity*." That made him laugh, too.

"Nobody ends up doing what they wanted to do."

He asked me about Brian Palmetto. In the past we used to argue about politics, he was definitely on the Ocasio-Cortez side of the Democratic Party. I was fine with Joe Biden, that's as far as I needed to go. Anyway, I worried about starting a fight but Eric was actually sympathetic. He said, that's one of the reasons I had to get out of LA. Too many talented white guys getting nowhere. I couldn't tell if he was kidding, but he said no. All the money these days is in diversity; he still has friends in LA he keeps in touch with. Come on, I said. Just look at the Oscars. But he said, that's just the tip of the iceberg, the tip of the iceberg. I didn't know what he meant.

"Didn't I sell you a house on Carroll Street?" It was the woman at the pool table; she was talking to me. "Come on, help me out here," she said. Foegley Landscape was looking over at us. He had soft brown hair like a loose shower cap, I don't know why this image occurred to me. He was about six-four. "You had a little girl," she went on. "I didn't think the marriage would last."

"Excuse me?" I said.

"I'm just messing with you. How old is she now?" She rested her cue against the wall, which was covered in seven-inch records around a framed Milwaukee Brewers Robin Yount jersey.

"Who?"

"Your daughter."

"Eighteen. I just dropped her off at college."

"Wow," she said.

"I think you've got me mixed up with someone else."

"Help me out here," she said again. "Want to shoot some pool?"

So the three of us ended up playing cutthroat. I mean, my brother and me and this woman, Sharon Donnegan—that's how she introduced herself. She worked for Weichert Realtors. Foegley tried to argue with her but she said, "I'm sorry, I ran into some friends," and eventually he went over to the bar and watched us from there.

Eric never had much hand-eye coordination, that was one area of childhood he left to me. Even as a teenager, when he got in shape, he was a get-in-shape kind of kid and not really into sports. Sharon and I were roughly on the same level but she won the first two games, which gave Eric a lot of joy. He was drunk enough he said things like, look at you, getting beat by a girl, which he wouldn't have said sober. But he also liked calling her a girl, I think he thought it sounded flattering or flirtatious. "Where'd you learn to play like that?" he said, and she said, "My dad was in the Air Force. Every base had a table."

"How'd you end up here?"

"I guess I'm just lucky," she said.

I felt bad for Eric, I don't think she was interested. When he missed a shot he asked her what he was doing wrong. "Your back stroke is all over the place," she said, and he said, "Show me."

The waitress came and he ordered three more beers. I told him, somebody's got to drive us home, I don't mind drinking Coke. And Sharon wanted a hard seltzer.

"I'm sorry, I drink like a girl."

In the end, she took over the order, because Eric was having trouble making himself understood. He wasn't that drunk but he was trying to manage too many interactions at once. So he had another IPA, and I had a Coke, and she had a Vizzy. It was about ten o'clock at night, I'd been in the car all day, I wanted to go home—or at least to my kid brother's rented apartment, where I could sleep in my niece's bottom bunk. Eric said we need to play again, to maintain the honor of the Layward brothers.

"Are you guys brothers? You don't look alike," Sharon said.

"He's a lot older than me, he let himself go."

I think Sharon liked me; it's awkward to write this, but she gave me that impression. And maybe that's why, when Eric said, show me, she finally said, all right, line one up, and stood behind him with her hips against his ass and her hand on his elbow and slowly guided his cue. While giving me a look, maybe she wanted to make me jealous, I don't know. Stir up some kind of fraternal rivalry for her attentions. I couldn't tell if Eric was having a good night, letting off steam, or just descending deeper into unhappiness. He kept wanting to use my phone.

"Where's yours?"

"I don't carry a phone," he said.

"You don't *carry* a phone? It's not like a gun."

But he borrowed mine and started taking pictures— mostly of Sharon bending down over the table. I won the third game. "So what are you doing here?" she said, when Eric went to the bathroom.

"I don't know. I don't know what I'm doing. Seeing my brother."

"And then what?"

"Tomorrow I'm driving to Denver."

"What's in Denver?"

"A guy I used to play basketball with."

"Aren't you an open book."

He was in the bathroom a long time. "You want another drink, or you want to go somewhere else?" she said. For a second I wondered what it would be like. She had a pale face, which the lipstick made look even paler, and I could see, when I stood next to her, the soft white skin of her scalp between the grains of her hair. She was younger than Amy and obviously less attractive, but you got an energy from her, like she was still interested in what might happen next, which I didn't get from Amy anymore.

"I think I should take my brother home."

"You *think*?"

But that's what I suggested, when he came out of the bathroom. He looked pretty pale himself, he didn't look good. But he didn't want to go home. He said, "We can't abandon Sharon to the vicissitudes," in one of his theatrical voices. I don't know who he was channeling. Some English actor. "You've got a pretty good accent," Sharon said. "My mother is actually Scottish, at least, that's where she was born."

He tried a Scottish accent, but it wasn't really coming.

"Who is this guy?" Sharon said.

"He used to work in Hollywood."

"No kidding."

"Come on, Eric. Time to go home."

"You go, I'll stick around with . . . Sharon. We're having a good time. Everybody knows how to have a good time except you."

"I don't think she wants you to stick around."

"She can say what she wants," Eric said.

She looked at him, she looked at me. It was a Monday night in Kelly's Pub, she probably had work in the morning. I don't know who goes out on Monday night, or why.

"I think I should probably head out too," she said. "I just need to use . . ." and she did a little curtsey, "the Ladies' Room."

"Are you all right to drive?" I asked.

"I'm fine, I'm just around the corner."

"We can wait for you," Eric said.

"That's all right. You boys run along."

So we left.

In the parking lot, we had an argument about who should drive. I'd had two or three beers, Eric had probably had a couple more. Also, it affected him more than it affected me, he was a very skinny, very nervy person. Eventually Eric gave me the keys but he wanted to wait until Sharon came out, to make sure she was okay.

"I don't want to be the guy in the car again," I said, but we waited a minute and then drove home.

It's only five minutes, we probably should have walked. Maybe it would have sobered Eric up. As soon as we started driving, his mood fell off a cliff. He sat hugging the seatbelt and looking out of the window. I didn't actually know the way, I kept saying, you have to tell me where to go. We crossed over the river and I tried to follow it into town. He said, "You didn't have to put her on the spot like that."

"What are you talking about?"

"Everybody was having a good time."

"Eric, I don't think she was into you."

"So why'd she ask us to play?" After a minute he said, "You always think women are hitting on you."

"Come on, Eric."

"Didn't some woman ask you to her birthday party?"

When we were driving out to Granger I'd told him about Diane, cruising by her dad's place last night and watching the cars line up, and feeling like, wherever you go you see this reality that you're outside of.

"I was just talking, it was just something to say."

"You were always like that, even when we were kids. You always thought other people were embarrassed by us."

By us I guess he meant Mom and him. "That's not true at all." But I don't know, maybe it was. He was twelve years old when I left for college, I didn't really know him as anything other than a fat little kid. He was always whining about something; I felt bad for him. He just wanted and wanted and didn't get, until Mom gave in. Sometimes I tried to distract the conversation from their constant interplay. I tried to get Mom to teach him self-restraint. But he didn't change until I left.

All that was thirty-five years ago. At a certain point with these family dynamics, you'd think the statute of limitations would run out.

We parked in the underground garage, which had an elevator. It was almost midnight, I don't think we talked. Back in his apartment, he said, "Do you need me to change the sheets? They're pretty clean. Anyway, you already slept in them."

"No, that's fine. Hey, it's nice to see you."

"Yeah."

"I'm sorry if I got it wrong tonight. I'm getting a lot of things wrong right now."

We were in the girls' bedroom. He sat down on one of the small chairs.

"I don't meet many women these days. I'm spending a lot of time in my own head."

"What about this job in Chicago?"

"How can I leave the kids?"

"They'll be all right. We were all right."

"It was all right for you," he said.

"You turned into a totally different person. You got your shit together. I can't tell you . . . how impressed I was, every time I came home. I thought, if he can do that to himself, he can . . . he'll be fine."

He looked at me with tears in his eyes. "I just miss having a woman in my life. I miss having somebody to be nice to."

"You've got the girls."

"That's pretty much my only function right now."

"No. No."

But I didn't know what else to say. He let me use the bathroom first, and then I lay in bed with the lights off and listened to him moving around. Eric warned me he wasn't much of a sleeper, he watched a lot of TV.

Lying there in the kids' bed, with the top bunk crowding down on me, I remembered something my dad once did. When I was about twelve years old, he took me out to Cadwalader Park to have a sex talk. We had just moved to Trenton, I thought he wanted to show me the neighborhood. But he explained about wet dreams, we talked about masturbation. Everything you think or want turns out to be normal, don't worry about that, he said. I was twelve, none of these biological changes meant much to me. Look, this is just a stage you have to go through. I'm sorry about it but there's nothing you can do. You just have to go through it. I tried to concentrate on my jump shot. If

I missed at least it gave me a minute to chase down the ball.

I'll give you some free advice, which you're not going to listen to, my dad said. But I listened. At some point you have to learn to control the sex urge, otherwise you let yourself get bossed around.

Who was he talking to? Me? By this point he was already having an affair.

He died in February 2020, just before everything shut down. Complications from diabetes; I don't really know what he died from. He had a stroke, then he went to the hospital and never came out. I always thought he looked after himself pretty well, for a man of his generation; his wife was somebody you could trust to be on top of things, medically. In spite of the way he left us he was basically a conservative person, who was always trying to protect himself against things going wrong. Walking out on Mom was the one big romantic gesture of his life.

Eric and I shared a hotel room, none of our wives or kids came to the funeral. We stayed at the Ramada, just off Route 55 and about ten blocks from the beach.

It was a very alienating experience. Everybody else at the funeral—he was cremated and half his ashes were scattered off a boat deck into the Pacific—belonged to his California life, his second life. (Later they erected a gravestone in Pacific View Memorial Park, where Kobe Bryant is also buried, but that was after we left.) We had two half sisters we barely knew, who were now thirty-something women and much closer to Dad than we ever were. The younger one, Sammy, wore a Philadelphia Eagles hard hat to the ceremony, the kind where you can strap a couple cans of beer or soda to the ear holes and drink them through a crazy straw without moving your head. It seemed inappropriate to me, Eric was very upset. It turned out Sammy had given Dad the hat for his birthday; he still rooted for Philadelphia sports teams and used to wear it in front of the TV on Sunday afternoons.

"What'd he drink?" I asked her.

"He didn't really fill it up, it was just for shits and giggles."

"I didn't even know he was a football fan."

"Oh he loved the Eagles, he watched every game."

She was the kind of person who is determined to have a good time at a funeral, because it's supposed to be a celebration of a happy life. Even if I'd had no personal connection to her, I don't think I would have liked her.

Because of jet lag, Eric and I woke up early after the funeral. Maybe we were both hungover. The heavy hotel curtains made it hard to tell the time of day. Eventually I got up (my bed was nearer the window) and pulled them back. So from about half past four we watched the California light slowly grade into morning. The traffic noise increased. We dozed a little, we looked at our phones. It was a long night. Eric said, "From their point of view, I don't think we ever really existed." And I told him, which I probably shouldn't have, the story of those last few weeks before Dad walked out.

"He told me he was going," I said. "He wanted to tell you, but you were too little, he thought you might tell Mom."

"But he knew you wouldn't."

"I guess he knew I wouldn't."

"What did you say?"

"I don't know, I don't remember. But I'll tell you a terrible thing, I felt excited for him. He was very excited, that's why he told me. He couldn't keep it a secret anymore, from all of us. He had to tell someone. Maybe I was just excited because it was me. I was fourteen years old. It just seemed like . . . one of those glimpses of adult life, which at that age . . . I wanted to know what was really going on. That's how it felt to me, but I also don't think . . . I didn't think he'd actually do it. When he left I was so ashamed, I couldn't even look at Mom. She thought I was upset because of Dad but really I just felt guilty. Have I told you this before? I don't think I've told anyone, except Jill."

"No, you didn't tell me. I'm sorry," Eric said.

"Why are you sorry?"

"That you had to deal with all that, it wasn't fair."

It's not what I expected him to say. I thought he'd be mad or jealous.

Later he said, "Why Jill?"

"I don't know. It just seemed like one of those things you tell your college girlfriend."

We had different flights out—I was going to JFK from LAX, he'd flown in to John Wayne. They had direct flights to Chicago, where he left the car. After that it was just a

136

two-hour drive to South Bend. We had breakfast together in the hotel restaurant then got different cabs. That was the last time I saw him, before now.

In the morning, I could tell the atmosphere had shifted. Whatever window of communication had opened up between us had closed again. It was just another working day, he liked to leave the house by eight o'clock. I was still in boxer shorts when I walked in.

"What happened to you?"

He was making coffee in the kitchenette. The toaster popped.

"I don't know. It's just something that started happening."

I guess he meant my face, which was swollen and leaking water through the eyes—I had to squeeze them just to see.

"Have you been to a doctor?"

"Of course I've been."

"What'd he say?"

"He thought I might be middle-aged."

"That was his diagnosis?"

"Eventually. They ran a lot of tests. I don't want to talk about it anymore."

"You need to do something." He felt happier, showing his concern.

"I know."

I drank some of the coffee he made and put another waffle in the toaster. There were a couple of stools under the kitchen counter. If you sat with your back against it, you could see the river. Funny how the eye is drawn toward water—it's just a very flat part of the view. But it shifts a little, slowly. Eric had disappeared into the bathroom. When he came out again, he looked like one of those people you meet whose job it is to be friendly and helpful. With his pale almost clean-shaven head and the Adam's apple in his neck.

He stood in the living-room area, and I got up to hug him but stopped a little short—he carried a messenger bag across his chest.

"Just close the door behind you," he said. "Are you coming back this way?"

"What do you mean?"

"After Denver . . . presumably you've got to get the car back to New York."

"I haven't really thought that far in advance."

"Well, if you do, you know where I live."

"It's good to see you, Eric. I hate to . . . I don't know, I hate all the distances."

"Well, this is America."

"Where should I put the presents for the girls?"

"Just leave them in their room. If it's candy their mother won't like it, but that's her problem."

After he left, I stacked the breakfast things in the dishwasher and showered—he only had one bathroom. There were rubber letters stuck to the side of the tub. Then I stripped the bed and packed my backpack and left.

Driving out, I followed my phone for a while but then, outside Waterford, I stopped for gas and turned it off. It was pretty much just a straight shot west. I was thinking about Eric but at some point realized that I was talking to Amy about him. The whole time I felt like I was in communication with her. She said, how's your brother, and I said, not great. We went out to some bar and he got drunk. There was a pool table and we started playing pool with some woman. Eric got a little . . . he was very attentive, which I don't think was appreciated. I didn't like seeing that.

It's fine, right? He's single . . . he's allowed to try.

No, but it feeds into this whole dynamic we used to have, where I was . . .

What? What were you? Did she want *you* instead?

I don't know and I don't really care; she wasn't important. I'm just worried about Eric.

You worry because it makes you feel better about yourself. You always have to be the responsible one.

That's not fair, that's not true. I mean . . . look at me now.

She didn't have an answer to that. I stopped for lunch in Des Moines, the highway takes you right through the city. It was after two, I'd been living off Pop'ettes and Fritos. Just after the river, I took an exit and drove around downtown looking for somewhere to eat. At least it was easy to park. Most of the businesses had spaces out front. There was a bakery that also served food, and I sat in the window and ate a chicken salad. I figured, look after yourself a little. It had peaches and pecans. I drank an ice tea. It was about eighty degrees outside, just a perfect September day. All of the roads were wide and empty, most of the buildings were office space. Above and between them, you could see cloudless blue sky.

Nobody tells you what an intense experience loneliness is, how it has a lot of variations. Just hour by hour. It occurred to me, not for the first time, that the three months of Amy's affair must have been one of the most exciting periods of her life. From which I was excluded, although maybe she felt like I was part of it, too. What happened was this. For several years in the buildup, we'd been arguing about a third child. Amy wanted another baby, I thought she needed to figure out what to do with her life. Because even another baby was only a temporary solution. She won the argument, but it didn't matter. For some reason she couldn't get pregnant and I wasn't willing to go through the whole IVF thing for the sake of . . . a child I had mixed feelings about.

That's not your problem, Amy said. You don't really have to go through anything. I'm the one who has to inject myself with hCG. Which is true. But it's expensive—I didn't care about the money—but it also requires a lot of coordination and organization and interaction, just the endless medical appointments and conversations, and at that point in our marriage we didn't have the resources for it, which I think she realized. So we didn't pursue it. But she came off the pill and didn't come back on. Her periods were always heavy; every month it was like another reproach. She explained to me once, it made her feel guilty, all those wasted eggs. And as I said before, her way of processing guilt was to turn it into anger, most of which was directed at herself, but there was enough left over for me to get my share.

While all this was going on, she got involved in the Jewish Book Council, which had its headquarters in Manhattan. Zach Zirsky put her on to it; he was a man of many sidelines. Every year the JBC ran an event to coincide with BookExpo America. They invited Jewish authors and Book Fair organizers to come together in one place so they could check each other out. There was an event, at some midtown hotel, where writers presented their books to a roomful of festival organizers, from places like San Diego and Pittsburgh and . . . Des Moines. For a lot of these people this counted as one of the perks of the job—going to New York for a few days, all expenses paid. They booked out the Algonquin on 44th Street, near Times Square. The atmosphere was like an academic conference, in which people get unreasonably excited about being away from home.

Amy obviously didn't have to stay over. The last train from Grand Central, which was three blocks away, left around 2 a.m. But she threw herself into the event like it was a real job, which paid actual money. She liked being part of a team; I'm sorry, I don't mean to sound about it the way I probably sound. Anyway, she wanted the full experience, and the JBC offered to pay for a room at the Algonquin so she could stick around for the cocktail party and help facilitate. Afterward, some of the writers and organizers went out for another drink, at the Twins Irish Pub on Ninth Avenue, where you could also get something to eat. Amy hadn't eaten all day, except for canapés, but the kitchen turned out to be closed.

Dara Horn was part of the gang, one of her favorite writers.

By the time she got back to the hotel, with Zach, who was there too, she must have been pretty drunk, which doesn't excuse what happened but partly explains it. Also, she'd been on a nervous high all day and used to get scared of what came after, which she didn't want to face. Just her ordinary life. So she wanted to keep the feeling going.

In the morning, she came home hungover. I remember picking her up from the station with the kids in the car. It was Saturday, we went out for pancakes. Amy said the whole event was pretty gruesome, writers writing about terrible things, the Holocaust, suicide, cancer, trying to sell their books like guests on Johnny Carson. After a minute, a bell dinged, and thirty seconds later they were ushered off the stage. She was very hungry, she finished Miri's eggs. It would have been just a one-night stand, which she could either tell me about or not, except that she turned out to be pregnant. This gave her an ongoing secret that she needed to communicate about with Zach, it was a reason to keep the relationship going. Because she genuinely didn't know what to do. She couldn't even be totally sure whose kid it was. But one thing she knew was she didn't want to have an abortion.

Three months later, she miscarried, and in the misery of that, couldn't keep secrets from me anymore. At least it meant she put an end to the affair, which she says she never really wanted in the first place. That much was a relief. Zach turned out to be a very needy and controlling person. He was also paranoid that his wife would find out, because she'd just kick him out, which is what eventually happened. I'm on thin ice already, he said. He actually moved back into his parents' house in Riverdale, so when his kids came to stay on the weekend that was who they stayed with, their father who was living with his parents in his childhood home. I didn't take comfort from this.

But for three months she was on the ice with him, living intensely from day to day, and for much of that time I had no idea.

"What would you have done if you'd had the baby?" This was one of our many circular conversations.

"I don't know," she said. "I can't explain it to you. After a while it felt like . . . he never made me do anything I didn't want to do, but that's what it felt like. Like I had to keep this affair going, for the baby. Even though he knew I didn't like him that much. It was a bad situation. I always loved you," she said, "even when I was . . . even if that's not how I behaved. I love you more than I love myself. That's just something I have to live with."

"What am I supposed to say to that," I said.

There's not a hell of a lot between Des Moines and Denver. I stopped for the night in a town called Ogallala. It had one of those cowboy Main Streets, with lit-up wooden signs— café/museum/gift shop/saloon. In other words, it looked like a Hollywood stage set for a frontier town, because in both cases there isn't much going on behind the frontage. Everything was closed at nine o'clock, even the saloon. But I found a room at the Quality Inn, where the desk guy pointed me to Casey's General Store, which served pizza. You could walk there from the hotel, along Chuckwagon Road. It ran parallel to the access road, with nothing but flat open grassland on either side. So that's what I did.

It was a mild night, the highway traffic was just another summer noise. I didn't feel particularly unhappy.

In the morning I drove to Denver to see Brian and arrived around lunchtime. Since he got fired he tended to eat at home; I had never been to his house before. He lived in Cherry Hills, one of those neighborhoods where you can't see the houses from the road. Trees get in the way, brick walls get in the way, yards on the scale of farmland get in the way. To find him I had to turn on my phone, and every time I did that, I got a buzz of anticipation or anxiety in case somebody had tried to get in touch. Michael left me a message every couple of days, which said, just checking in—fulfilling a conscientious duty. But I also had an email from Amy.

It was a link to a real estate listing for a two-bed co-op on E. 81st, just a few blocks from where we used to live. No other comment so I clicked the link. Full service doorman, roof garden, swimming pool, gym. The apartment had its own private terrace overlooking York Avenue. It cost a million dollars, which was maybe what we could get for our house in Westchester, if we were lucky.

A few years ago we talked about moving to the city when Miri left home; at least, Amy talked about it. I couldn't tell if this was a reference to that conversation or something else. Maybe she wanted a place for herself, in case we split up; she still had a pot of inheritance from her father's death. Obviously, these are very different messages. Even though I had this idea that I was communicating with Amy the whole time, it was just an idea in my head that I was talking to and not the actual person, who was going through her own . . . transitions. So who knows. I read the message after pulling up outside Brian's house, then I got out of the car and rang the buzzer by the wide front gate.

Brian met me in the yard. The walk to the front door was like crossing a football field. There were pine trees in the grass, and the house behind it looked like a prison, with small windows and high brick walls. At that distance, you have an awkward delay between seeing each other and having to interact. Meanwhile, you keep walking. "Yo yo yo," he said, about twenty yards away. In his playing days he was listed at six-six, two-twenty, these days he was a little heavier. But he still had the old strawberry-and-cream complexion. He's one of those fair-haired Italians. Being hugged by him made me feel like a girl or a kid.

I should probably say a word about our friendship. From sophomore year, we roomed together, not just on campus but for road games too. He was maybe the second-best player on the team, although that's arguable; he may also have been the best. (Our star was a six-two shooting guard named Aldiss Bletchley, who played professionally in Israel for a few years after graduating. Now he's a management consultant in the Dallas/Fort Worth area, unless he's already retired to play golf.) I was the eighth or ninth man. The only reason I got any playing time was because I could shoot, and Brian liked playing with me. He was kind of an early point forward, who orchestrated the offense from the low post—he used to finish games with stat lines like, eight points, eleven rebounds, seven assists. I mention this stuff because it shaped our relationship. He was the guy who let me tag along, and I was the guy at the back of the bus who amused him by making snide remarks.

In general, he saw me as his intellectual friend, which . . . in no other company did I qualify. I had a steady girlfriend (Jill loved him), while Brian went through a lot of one-night stands. I mean, there were other ways in which the power-dynamic was more balanced. Sometimes I even got a vague feeling that on some level . . . I'm not expressing myself well. Once, working out in the Pitzer gym, we were in the weight room, spotting each other on the bench press. After a set, in front of the wide tall mirrors, he put his arm around my shoulder and said, "If only I could meet a girl, who was like a normal girl and six foot two."

I didn't have a response to this. I never saw him together with a guy but he was generally a very sexual person. Somehow he had a reputation as a skirt-chaser but women liked him, too. He had close female friends who knew that if he got drunk he might try to kiss them (I think he made a pass at Jill once, too), but because he didn't mind when they turned him down, they didn't seem to mind either.

It was great to see him. Nothing ever changed when you saw him, we were still twenty years old, a couple of guys. But I knew within five minutes that I wouldn't open up to him about anything.

He was making lunch when I showed up, big sandwiches. The kitchen counter was spread with mayo, mustards, pickles, chilies and cold cuts, various cheeses and breads. He had a panini maker and a juicer on the go. At four o'clock, he said, I have to pick up Evelyn from school. I'm turning into daddy day care. Ricky drives himself, can you believe it, we bought him a secondhand Bolt for his sixteenth birthday, and Molly usually gets a ride with him. Unless she has volleyball, which she sometimes does. But until then, I'm a free agent. What do you want to do. Help yourself. Let's eat.

This was what it was like, you followed in his wake.

When I got there I didn't know how long I'd stay, but I ended up staying only twenty-four hours. For no particular reason, except that I realized somewhere in the course of the day that I didn't want to hang out in someone else's homelife. I had a kind of momentum on the road that was a useful distraction. But basically I had a good time.

After lunch he showed me the house and the yard. It wasn't my kind of house, but I could see he spent a lot of money on it. It's funny, I sometimes got intimations of Amy's reactions to things, which were now my reactions.

The Naftalis have very good taste, modest and old-fashioned. They only show off in code, you have to know what you're looking for. But where Brian spent money you could always tell.

There was a tennis court in the yard, with a basketball hoop at one end. We shot around and I mentioned my old dumb idea for a book about pickup basketball, which was turning into something I could talk to people about, because it didn't matter and it wasn't going to happen. But Brian got excited about it. He was a member of the Colorado Athletic Club but realized that's not the kind of America I had in mind. Anyway, he said, I prefer to play where the brothers play. So we got in his car (a Tesla Model X) and drove out of the compound and through the wide empty streets of Cherry Hills, heading downtown.

I liked looking around. Brian was easy to talk to, because he did most of the talking.

He said he didn't play much anymore, back, knees, feet. But fuck it, we're only getting older, it's only gonna get worse. I said we don't have to play, I can just take pictures. And I tried to tell him about my collection of symptoms. "Sometimes when I run, it's like ... they pulled the plug, I totally run out of gas. My head feels funny, too. I get little blackouts."

"Believe me," he said, "I don't plan on running much."

But we talked about Todd Gimmell too. I said I wanted to meet him (which wasn't true), but Todd had gone to LA. He was hoping to make the Clippers training camp. A lot of guys work out at UCLA over the summer.

"It's good to see you," Brian said. He said this several times. "It's been a tough few months. Sometimes I don't know what people do all day."

We drove to Lawson Park, in the middle of Five Points. It had a kiddy playground, a baseball diamond, and an asphalt half-court. Opposite was a grand old yellow-brick building called The Absolute Word Church. It was about two thirty in the afternoon, and three guys were shooting around— mid-twenties, in matching overalls. The biggest one was maybe six-four; even in his work shoes he could dunk.

"Can you still dunk," I said to Brian.

"Fuck no."

I walked around taking pictures on my phone, and feeling like a fraud. When you live secretly it puts you in a lot of these positions, where you end up doing things you have no real conviction about. But fine, whatever, you just have to get through it.

When I came back, Brian had challenged them to a game. (Before we left, I'd changed into running shorts; he'd been wearing sweatpants all day.) "How do you want to do this," one of them said. Everybody introduced themselves: Sean, Wayman, and a guy whose name I didn't catch. Brian said, "I'm happy with two on three."

"Well, we can sub somebody out."

So that's what we did. It was half-court so nobody had to run much. I hadn't played with Brian in thirty years but he made it easy. When he set a pick, he really set a pick. On the first play of the game, I walked into a lay-up. He had quick hands, too, and even if he didn't move his feet, he liked to swipe down hard on the ball, so it made a popping sound when he hit it. He got a couple of steals that way. On offense he just backed his man down; they had to double-team him, which left me open for fifteen-footers. I'd been shooting almost every day, these are not hard shots.

They subbed the big man in, but it made no difference. Brian knew how to play, these guys were just bangers. He liked to talk too, but in a friendly way—the whole time he was kicking their ass, he complained about his feet. I'm not sure I saw him jump six inches off the ground. But you forget what it's like to play with somebody who really knows what he's doing. The world just opens up.

It was a friendly game. Guys recognize the real thing when they see it. I had a good time, I hit a lot of shots. We only played about half an hour. They worked for a limousine service a couple of blocks away and had to get back to work. Brian said, "Can we take a picture with you guys? My buddy here is writing a book."

So there's a picture of me against the hoop at Lawson Park, standing next to Brian and Wayman. Brian has his arm around me; I'm trying to palm the basketball. Sometimes, sitting in the hospital chair, I think about that afternoon, and tell myself, maybe again.

Afterward, we had to pick up Evelyn from school, which was just about a ten-minute drive from Brian's house. And then family life took over. Tandy, his wife, came home around six o'clock. Tandy is just her nickname; she's half-Filipino, her real name is Tadhana. As it happens, she's about five foot nothing. She works for the Nuggets too, which is where Brian met her. She started dancing for them in college, then after graduation got a job in the PR department. The Nuggets Dancers are like their own mini-organization, you can book them for events. They have a high turnover too, which means it's a lot of work trying to maintain some kind of identity.

Things got uncomfortable when the Nuggets fired Brian, but they decided Tandy should stick with it until he figured out what to do next. "So I'm a househusband now," he said, but from what I saw, she pretty much took over after getting home. Cooking dinner, yelling at the kids about their homework. Brian and I retreated to the games room. But maybe that was just because he had a friend over, who knows. I wasn't in a position to judge other people's marriage arrangements.

So these are some of the things we talked about. "How's Amy," he said, and I said, "Fine. A little heartbroken about Miri; she wanted to come along but couldn't face it."

"Don't," Brian said. "I don't want to think about it. Though honestly it might be a relief when Ricky moves out. He's a pain in the neck. At least with me; he's nice to his sisters."

Later he told me, "Last summer Molly started spending a lot of time in the bathroom. That's the problem with a big house, you never know what's going on. But the pandemic hit her pretty hard, she was a very social girl. And suddenly all that was taken away. The only person she talked to about it was Ricky."

"What was she doing in there?"

"Nothing really, she was just . . . experimenting with experimenting, that's what Tandy says. I never actually had a conversation with Molly about it, she didn't want to talk to me. Nobody tells me anything. They think . . . Tandy says I don't really understand what anybody goes through. I never had a problem you couldn't solve by going to the gym. I don't even know if that's true. But Molly was always . . . Daddy's little girl, she didn't want to disappoint me. Tandy thought it might be better if she thought I didn't know."

I said, "I'm sorry."

Dinner was potluck stir-fry. It had a family name I don't remember, they called it something different. Tandy laid out options on the counter, this seemed like a Palmetto thing. The kids could pick what they wanted, and she fried it up, which meant spending half the meal next to the stove. She said she didn't mind. I never knew her well, but Tandy always struck me as one of those people whose cheerfulness is about three feet thick. Ricky liked pork belly but Molly was a vegetarian, so her mother cleaned the wok for her in-between. Afterward, the kids cleared the table and Brian and I went back to the games room.

It had a pool table and an air hockey table and a couple of arcade games. Pool is one of the few games I can beat him at, so we played pool. Brian was always generous like that. He was super competitive but not with me. In college, I was the guy he told stuff to.

At one point he said, "I didn't think we'd end up like this."

"Like what?"

"Come on, Tom. Don't make me say it."

"Say what?"

"Hiding in my room. That's what it feels like, at least. You know what I mean."

"Not really."

"Half the things I think are true, my kids think make me an asshole. Even Ricky. You know, he's never had a girlfriend. He's seventeen years old. I don't even know if he likes girls. If I say to him, what about so-and-so, he acts like I'm being disgusting. I mean, somebody has to go out with somebody, eventually, right? Or have we just given up on all that?"

"Maybe it's better if we give up on it."

"When I was his age, let me tell you, I was having a lot of fun."

He asked me about Jill, too. He said, "When's the last time you heard from her?"

"I don't know. Ten years ago. Maybe more. When her daughter was born."

After hitting forty, Jill decided to have a baby. She had never gotten married, a couple of long-term relationships didn't pan out, so she went to a sperm bank and bought some sperm. I don't remember the details but she was totally forthcoming. There are all kinds of human qualities you get to choose from. Anyway, she had a baby girl. But it was around the same time Amy had her affair, I wasn't really responding to other people. Jill must have been pretty busy too. We fell out of touch.

"She sent me an email a few weeks ago, when the Kirkland story came out. I think she still hangs out with people from the sports desk."

"How's she doing?"

"Not great. She was seeing a guy but it ended. The pandemic . . . they closed all the schools in Las Vegas, too. We were just lucky Tandy could take time off."

"I'm sorry," I said.

"Well, it's not your fault. She says she's doing better, that's not why she got in touch."

"Maybe I can stop off on the way to LA."

Most of what we talked about was his lawsuit. At some point I told him I was driving to Los Angeles to see Michael; Brian made me promise to look up Todd Gimmell. "He's a real out-there kid. I think you'll like him. Well, I don't know. But he doesn't care what anybody thinks about him anyway."

Right now, Brian was just in the process of gathering signatories. Todd was helping him with that, too—anybody who was in the league, or out of it, or on the fringes, who had a story to tell about discrimination against white players. But there's a whole . . . thin blue line situation. Even ex-players don't like to talk about it, a lot of them are in the media. "But I mean, just look at the numbers," Brian said. "More than sixty percent of Div 1 college basketball players are white . . . that's the main recruiting ground for the NBA. But less than twenty-five percent of NBA guys are white, and a lot of those are actually European."

"There may be a simple explanation for that," I said.

"Come on, you don't even believe that. Just look at the way the media talks about white players. Imagine a business where ten percent of the population makes up eighty percent of the workforce, where people are making millions and millions of dollars . . . you'd think something was going on. Europe is a totally different culture, those guys don't feel like they have to apologize all the time, which is why all the white talent in the league is coming from overseas. But if you're a white kid in America, the hill is just too big to climb."

What could I say to him? For three years we shared a bedroom and sometimes stayed up talking till 4 a.m. If I looked hard I could see, under his old face, the shape of someone more elderly starting to push through—the skin of his neck had softened; his yellow hair was less yellow. It was harder for him to get out of a chair. He drank two bottles of Michelob Ultra at dinner and then opened a couple more in the rec room afterward. When I didn't touch mine, he finished it, and opened another. There was a fridge next to the pinball machine. But he never seemed remotely drunk, he was just drinking. In college he drank a lot, too. I don't know if he'd actually changed that much. But in those days you never really felt any . . . heat of complaint coming off him, he was having too much fun. Which obviously wasn't the case right now.

"You've got great kids," I said, to change the conversation.

"Well, they were showing off for you. Molly's the only one who cares about any of the things I care about . . . but that's not their fault."

"I may have left Amy."

I don't know why I said it. If you take in all these confessions, after a while you feel like, it's your round. But then as soon as I said it, I knew I had betrayed her. Brian never liked Amy; he thought she was a snob.

"Oh," he said.

"I don't really know what I'm doing. When I dropped off Miri, I just kept going."

"Listen," he said. He was getting excited now. "Stay as long as you want. You can see for yourself . . . I'm not doing anything. You can stay in the pool house, we've got a guest room there. You won't even have to see anybody. Just hang out when you want to."

Tandy came in around eleven to say good night. Brian had said, "You don't care if he stays for a few weeks? He just needs a little time to . . . he's trying to figure a few things out."

"Of course not," she said. "He can stay in the pool house." And then, to me: "Take this guy off my hands. You'd be doing us a favor."

"Well, I don't know. That's very kind. I have to make a few phone calls."

"Not tonight."

"No, not tonight."

After she left, we played another game of pool; Brian made me drink another beer. It touched me, to see how pleased he was, even if I felt like, you don't even know me anymore. We're just acting like this because we think it's how old friends are supposed to act. But maybe other people don't feel like this, maybe it's just me. There was a seventy-inch TV screen mounted on the wall, and at midnight, he started flicking through channels. One of the Bourne movies was on, I don't remember which one. "I can't sleep anyway," Brian said. "What the hell, right? It's not like we've got anything to get up for."

But I said, "I'm beat," and eventually he let me go to bed.

In the morning, there was the usual rush, but not much of it involved Brian. Ricky and Molly drove to school together, Tandy dropped off Evelyn on the way to work. I was aware of being a dim presence in the background of the more vivid lives of children. After they left, I went for a run; Brian, to save his knees, worked out on the rowing machine. To get to the park, you have to cross over a highway. I stopped a lot and walked and sat on benches, and ran a little farther.

When I got back, I told him I wanted to drive on. I wanted to see Michael and visit my dad's grave in Newport Beach. He only let me leave because I agreed to meet with Todd Gimmell in LA.

KVOQ was on the radio when I drove out, and they were playing Townes Van Zandt: *Well, I'm going out to Denver . . . see if I can't find . . . that lovin' Colorado girl of mine . . .* I turned onto 285 and then hit some crazy spaghetti junction and looped back onto I-70. Which I then followed for many, many miles, while the country shifted around me, from fir trees and green hills and distant mountains to the weird red landscape of Utah. It was like a science-fiction movie. I kept thinking, who says God has no imagination . . . Nobody . . . Hard to believe in a population problem in the middle of all *this*. But you'd need a space station to live here. I don't know who I was talking to in my head, maybe Miri. The dashboard thermometer read a hundred two, a hundred and three. From time to time train tracks ran along the highway, I couldn't always tell if the freight cars were moving. It felt a bit like seeing three-masted ships.

I was hoping to make it to Las Vegas but came off the interstate at a town called Mesquite around eight o'clock. Most of the hotels had casinos attached. I think I'd already crossed into Nevada.

Something upsetting happened in Mesquite. The desk clerk recommended a place called Peggy Sue's; you had to drive to get there, because you had to drive everywhere. Outside the hotel it was all highways and five-lane roads. A dust storm had blown in, and the sunset looked like gas flares coming out of the hills. I mention these things only to say that I was already disoriented.

After driving all day, I got back in the car—it was only five minutes away.

There was a public park about a block from the restaurant. I missed the turnoff and ended up pulling over to check my phone. I worried I was already too late, most of these places shut at nine o'clock. But some kind of festival was going on. I could hear a PA system; the parking lot was full of cars. People sat in the grass or on foldout chairs around a squared-off enclosure. Inside it, dancing was going on, women and children in Native American costumes, in feathers and beads. The music sounded like chanting, but it was all recorded. I couldn't see anyone singing.

I said, "What's going on?" to a guy selling cans of soda from a little cooler you could wheel around.

"Dancing."

"Is it . . . a religious festival?"

"A competition. Every Thursday."

Maybe I misunderstood him, the music was very loud. I left the car and started to run back toward the restaurant, when someone said, "Excuse me."

A girl was sitting on the curb, next to a skateboard.

"Hey." I stopped running.

"Can you help me?" she asked, standing up. "I had an accident."

She looked about seventeen years old, maybe older. It was hard to tell. She wore denim shorts and a T-shirt that was much too big for her; she had straight black hair. The way she spoke, I couldn't tell if English was her first language. But there was no accent, she just had a very flat way of speaking. I couldn't see any bruises or cuts on her arms or legs.

"You all right?"

"I think I dislocated my shoulder." But she didn't sound in pain.

"There's a restaurant over there . . . why don't you sit down, they can call an ambulance. You can have a glass of water."

"Can you drive me home?" she said. "It's only six blocks."

"Where are you staying?"

And she pointed along the five-lane road, back toward the highway. "At the motel."

"Is your family there?"

She shook her head.

"Do you live there?"

"You can pay by the month."

"If you're hurt, you should see a doctor."

"I just want to go home."

I felt like telling her, don't get in cars with strange men. But it wasn't for me to say. I also thought, this is a scam, but couldn't figure out the trick.

"Can you give me a ride?" she said again.

Meanwhile, wind blew dust along the road, and over the sound of it, you could hear the PA system. I'd been driving all day, all week, I was in the middle of nowhere, and felt like, there are things going on under the surface that you have no idea about.

"I'm sorry," I said. "I can't."

"I saw you get out of the car."

"I can't. I've got to . . . I'm late already."

"It's only six blocks." But she wasn't pleading, she didn't sound disappointed. She was just stating facts.

"I'm sorry," I said.

It was ten to nine when I made it to the restaurant. The waiter was stacking chairs and the tiles were wet. But they let me order the meatloaf and a bottle of beer. I sat at the counter and ate as fast as I could. The whole time I kept thinking, she's going to steal my car. For no particular reason, at least nothing I could put my finger on, I felt scared of this seventeen-year-old girl. Maybe she was turning tricks, or back at the motel she had a couple of guys waiting for me. Or maybe she hurt herself skateboarding, I don't know.

By the time I got to the parking lot, the dancing was over. Some people were loading up one of the trucks. My car was fine. I drove back to the hotel and lay in the stiff sheets feeling guilty.

It was only about an hour to Las Vegas, but I wasted most of the morning at the hotel . . . running on the treadmill, swimming in the pool, and losing fifty bucks at the roulette tables. That was what I walked in with. I bought the chips and left when they were gone. Then I had lunch at the casino and drove off.

I reached Jill's house around three o'clock. She lived in Paradise Palms, about ten minutes off the highway. I don't know Vegas at all, I followed my phone. Brian had given me her address. The house was a cute fifties bungalow with green-trimmed windows, a white picket fence, and one of those old car ports next to the door, which is just a roof you drive under. The front yard was mostly gravel. It had a small circular flower bed in the middle, walled off with rusty fenders, and a century plant growing out of it. It was the kind of house I imagined she might have, and it was nice to think that she was living according to her tastes, and that they hadn't changed much.

The street itself was wide and flat, the sky over my head was wide and flat and blue; it was about a hundred degrees outside. There wasn't any shade, except for Jill's car port, which I stood underneath while ringing the bell. Even in the shade the heat had a kind of pulse; you could smell the baked concrete. Her front door had glass panels but they were covered in blinds.

Nobody was home. I figured, at some point she has to pick her daughter up from school. So I went back to the car, which was starting to heat up rapidly now that the engine was off. Maybe this is why I fell asleep. For months, I'd been sleeping badly, getting up several times a night to piss. Being on the road didn't help. I don't sleep well on first nights, and lately I'd been having a lot of first nights. So I pushed back the driver's seat and thought, you should probably get her something, why don't you drive around and find a supermarket. They might have flowers. You should buy something for her daughter too. This was still going through my head when she woke me up, tapping on the glass.

"Hey," she said.

After that the whole afternoon had a post-nap flavor of unreality.

It was after four, I must have been asleep for an hour. Jill's daughter was named Katie, she seemed excited to have a man in the house. At least this was what Jill said. She made peanut butter and banana sandwiches for her after-school snack. I had one too, with a glass of milk. We sat at the Formica kitchen table, the floor was checkerboard linoleum, black

162

and white. The whole house had a fifties vibe, maybe a little too much.

Katie wanted to go swimming. While she got changed, Jill said, "What the hell are you doing here?"

"I don't really know. My son lives in LA. That's where I'm headed. I thought I'd stop in and see you on the way."

"How do you even know where I live?"

"Brian Palmetto told me."

Katie came down in her swimsuit, a red bikini. She must have been twelve years old but still looked like a kid. Jill said, "I should get changed too. Do you want a dip?"

"I don't have a swimsuit."

"I'm sure we can find you something."

But I ended up going out to the car and getting my backpack. My running shorts were basically swimming trunks, they had an inner lining. I changed in the downstairs bathroom. There was a stack of *National Geographic* magazines on the tank; I almost hit my head on the potted plant hanging in the window. It overlooked the backyard, which was just a concrete patio with a pool carved out of it, shaped like a kidney. Katie was already in the water. Jill lay on one of the deck chairs.

I walked outside barefoot on the hot stone and lay down next to her.

"This is the life," I said.

"Well, it's Friday afternoon." Later she said, "What the hell's going on? I haven't seen you in . . . twenty years, and then you just, you're sleeping in a car outside my house."

"I've become one of those guys."

"What guys?"

"The guys you see sitting in a parked car, and wonder, what are they hiding from."

"What are you hiding from?"

"Nothing, I'm just . . . I'm trying to write a book," I said.

So we talked about that for a while, and I felt like a phony. Katie kept calling for her mother to get in, and Jill said, "In a minute." She wore a silver one-piece and had come out in a pair of Havaianas, which lay by the deckchair. Her toenails were painted bright pink.

"What are you looking at?" she said. "I probably look really old."

"No. You look like you. At least to me."

"My mother always said, you can keep your face or your figure. It seemed like more fun keeping my face."

"You look great."

"Well, I could lose two or three or fifteen pounds. You don't have to respond to that," she said.

"You look a lot better than me."

"You don't look too bad." She turned over and rested on her elbow. We were lying close enough she could reach out and touch my chest. There was a network of broken veins under my heart, like blue in cheese.

"What's that?"

"I don't know, they just appeared."

"When?"

"A couple of months ago."

164

"Middle age is fun, right? I get the same on my legs."

And she rolled over to show me, little purple clusters on the backs of her knees. She was always one of those pretty girls who doesn't mind putting herself in a bad light.

"Your legs look fine."

"Tell that to Mr. Tinder," she said.

It was hot enough you didn't have to talk, you could just lie there. Eventually Jill got up and dived in, swam a length and got out again, then lay back wetly against the deck chair. She had a very pink complexion and even in college used to slather on sunscreen whenever the sun came out, which was most of the time in southern California. She didn't care what it looked like. Thirty years later, she was still like that, and I watched her reapply the sunscreen thickly to her face and shoulders and the triangle of chest not covered by her suit.

"Is that something you do?" I said.

"What?"

"Tinder."

"I did. I don't. You reach a point in your life where you don't want strangers in your life anymore. At least until Katie leaves home. Are you okay?"

"What do you mean?"

"Your heart. . ."

"I don't know. The doctors can't find anything wrong."

It was almost six o'clock, and the shade of the neighbor's house had started to stretch across the patio, covering my face. But it was still ninety-plus outside.

"I should probably get going," I said.

"It's too late to drive to LA."

"If I get tired, I can stop at a motel."

"Why don't you stay here?"

"Watch me, Mom," Katie called out. "I'm doing a fat bomb." And she ran off the edge and cannonballed into the water, trying to make us wet, and more or less succeeding.

"She just started using that word," Jill said.

"I don't know if it means anything."

"When a twelve-year-old girl uses it, it means something. You can sleep on the sofa bed. I'm meeting some people for dinner, but you can come too."

"If you want me to babysit . . ."

"I want you to come."

Then the kid climbed out and stood dripping over me.

"Do you have any money?"

"Watch out," Jill said.

"If you throw it in, I can dive for it."

My wallet was in my jeans, which I had laid in a pile of clothes next to the deck chair. I had to sit up to get it. Then I took out the change, a good handful, and tossed it in. Katie waited for everything to settle before diving down. Afterward, she lined the coins up carefully on the far side of the pool.

"Aren't you gonna swim?" she asked.

"Well, maybe to get my money back."

There was a bucket of goggles and other aquatic equipment next to the steps. I pulled out a pair, which were much too tight, and put them on. Then I walked around to the deep end and jumped in. The water was surprisingly cold, it took my breath away. I guess the desert gets cool at night and even a day of sunshine isn't enough to take the edge off. I swam hard for a minute then hoisted myself against the side of the pool and threw all the money back in, which made Katie jump on my back to try and stop me. The whole time, I was conscious of Jill looking on, watching her daughter with this man. All the coins scattered on the bottom. Diving down, I felt the pressure on my face, which persisted even when I rose to the surface again.

When I looked up, Jill was on her cell phone.

"Mom," Katie called out. "Hey, Mom."

"What?"

"Mom."

"I'm on the phone."

"Why's he gone that funny color?"

"Oh my God," Jill said. "Get out, get out, get out. You need to get out of the water. Get out now. Get out."

"Hey, hey," I said. "It's fine, I'm fine."

"I need to go now," she said and hung up. "Get out of the water, get out of the water." She was shouting at me, so I swam over to the steps and climbed out. It was a relief to take off the goggles.

"I'm calling an ambulance," she said. "Sit down. Just sit down."

"What's going on? I'm fine."

Eventually she put down her phone. "Look in the mirror."

So I walked into the house, tracking the wet with me; my face in the bathroom mirror looked blue, but that's all. There were deep lines against my cheeks where the goggles had cut in.

"What's going on?" I said, coming out again.

"Your whole . . . chest went purple, I thought you were going to die."

"I'm fine."

"God, you gave me a scare. Just . . . don't do anything, all right? Just sit down for a minute. You still look . . . just sit down."

"You can check my pulse."

And she put her hand to my heart. "It's fast," she said, and I touched my wrist.

"It's fine."

"Tom," she said. "All right, Katie. Time to get out . . ."

"Just five more minutes."

"I said, get out," she screamed.

The mood had shifted. This was turning into one of those evenings where the stakes are high, I can't explain it better. We weren't just making conversation anymore. Katie didn't say anything, getting out; she was in a huff, and all the change still lay on the bottom of the pool. The sun was setting across the low houses, you could feel the temperature skip a few degrees going down. Jill started to boil water and Katie said, "I don't want pasta," and Jill said, "Well, that's what I'm making."

I sat down dripping at the kitchen table, and Jill said, "If you want to have a shower, you can use my bathroom." I figured they probably needed a little space and took my time.

Afterward, Katie and I watched TV on the sofa while Jill got ready—*Friends* seemed to be on back to back. It's like the weather these days, always going on in the background. She said, "I didn't think you looked that bad. Mom always overreacts."

The babysitter came when Jill was still in her room. Her name was Vanessa, she was a grad student at UNLV. She brought a backpack with her and took out her computer and started setting up on the kitchen table. I asked her what she was studying, and she said, "Business administration."

"What does that entail?"

But then Jill came out, in a yellow dress and sandals. She always looked nice in a dress, because she still moved like the girl who captained her high-school volleyball team, and the dress let her show it.

"Hey, look at you," Vanessa said.

"What about me?"

The only thing I had to wear were jeans and old Converse, and I held in my hand the shirt I'd bought at Walmart in case the restaurant was over air-conditioned.

"You'll do," Jill said.

Before we left, she had to make up with Katie, but it didn't take long. Katie asked her, "How much TV can I watch?"

"It's Friday night, I don't really care. It's up to Vanessa."

"Vanessa doesn't care. Do you, Vanessa?"

"Just be in bed by ten, okay?"

"I love you," Katie said. Then we were out the door, in the early desert evening, under a pale blue sky.

We took Jill's car, a Subaru Forester, which looked fairly new. Financially, she seemed pretty comfortable. I said, "So who's going to be there tonight, who are these people?" Instead of answering, she leaned over and kissed me; her hair was still wet from the swim. Her perfume filled the car, we made out for a while.

"Just promise me you're not going to die tonight," she said.

"I'm not planning on it."

"I better start driving," she said. "We don't want to put on a show."

The restaurant was about twenty minutes away, you had to cross the highway to get there. I don't know what I was feeling, I couldn't tell you. Nothing in this city seemed very real. Everything we drove on turned out to be a six-lane road; eventually she pulled off into a strip mall. There was a USA Auto Service center, a liquor store, a nail salon, and a supermarket. All the architecture looked like dental offices, but we parked in front of one of them.

"Don't look so scared," she said. "These are all nice people."

"I'm not scared, I'm just kind of . . . out of it." And the first shadow fell across her mood.

Inside, the windows were covered with strips of white curtain; the color scheme was red and white. It was like a Japanese dive-bar, the menu was scribbled on a chalkboard against the wall. There was a bar at one end, and a lot of beat-up wooden tables, which were mostly empty even on a Friday night. Jill's friends had a table under one of the windows, but you couldn't see out, you might have been anywhere in the world.

After that it was just a . . . it was like a basketball game, everything happened faster than you could make sense of it. It was a performance. I said my name several times and repeated other people's names. There were three other couples, including a guy Jill knew from her days at the *Review-Journal*. He was still on the sports desk; his wife worked for the city. She was actually the person who helped Jill get a job at the Office of Community Affairs. So it's her fault, Jill said, that I have to go to Carson City six times a year. People said a lot of things that I didn't totally understand.

But I liked Daryl, the sports-desk guy. His special beat was gambling and sports, which had changed unrecognizably in the last few years. He had a likeable, unattractive face. His hair was thinning and his nose was pitted with old acne scars, but you also got the feeling, if he wanted a woman's attention he could get it. Jill said to him, "Tom's writing a book about pickup basketball," so for part of the meal I had to talk about that. "What's the idea," Daryl said, and I said, "I'm not really sure yet, it's just something I always wanted to do. Drive across the country and play pickup and write about the courts and the people you come across." So we talked a little about the Las Vegas basketball scene. "It doesn't really have those kinds of neighborhoods," he said. "The only place I ever played is Sunset Park, but that's like, just a very nice park. What people don't realize about Vegas is that it's a great hiking town."

Even though the restaurant was empty, the music was loud. Also, it was a small-plate kind of place, so we kept

171

ordering food—sashimi and hand rolls; they served unusual cocktails. I wondered if Jill would get drunk but she had one tequila cocktail (infused with hibiscus and Tajín, she let me taste it) and then stuck to bottled beer. From time to time I looked at her; I'm sure she did the same to me. She was a very familiar person but the familiarity was out of date, and I didn't know if it was still good, if it still counted. My general experience of ex-girlfriends is that some part of you is always attracted to them, regardless of what stage of life they're at or what they look like. But also, it doesn't matter very much, it's just one of those dumb facts about someone.

My main feeling was sadness, which I tried to cover up. I asked Daryl if he knew who Todd Gimmell was. He said he did. I told him I was supposed to interview him for a class-action suit, which my friend Brian Palmetto was trying to put together. He knew about Brian too, and said, "The way things went down in Denver was just a mess, it was ugly all round. Nobody comes out of it smelling like roses. But I wouldn't go near Todd Gimmell," he said. "I'm not even saying he's wrong, but I wouldn't touch him."

"Why not?" But we got interrupted by other conversations.

I thought, what if I moved in with Jill and became friends with these people, so that the last thirty years of our lives turned out to be just an interruption. Would Katie eventually think of me as her father? The thought made me ... it wasn't even a feeling of guilt, it was a deeper horror than that. (Miri, Michael.) I don't even mean that it seemed impossible, because this is basically what my dad did. There's almost nothing you can't do to yourself, that's what I thought. And whatever it is, you'll probably survive and maybe even end up happier than you were before. But that doesn't make it less terrible.

I wasn't drinking much, but I had a couple of those cocktails, which tasted like fruit juice but hit harder. After that, I thought, slow down and stuck to water.

Somebody asked me how we met, and Jill overheard and started telling the story. "We went to college together," she said. "And we both thought, I know, let's try acting . . ." She was laughing when she said it. "There was this semi-professional company that advertised on campus, because that way they could get college funding. Anyway, they were putting on *The Winter's Tale*, and we both tried out."

"My part was so small," I said, "the character didn't even have a name. Jill played Mopsa, a shepherdess."

"Wasn't I cute," she said. Other people were laughing too.

"But it was . . . it was actually kind of sad. One of the cast was this single mother, who seemed like unbelievably old, because she had a thirteen-year-old son. Anyway, she had to take him every night to rehearsals so he was always hanging around."

"He came out to Jill."

"He had a crush on Tom, and wrote him a long letter, and wanted me to give it to him."

"What did you do?"

"I gave it to him."

173

"Did you tell his mother?"

"No, we were just kids, we didn't know what to do. We didn't think it was funny, but . . . it's how we got together. It gave us something to talk about."

"That's the story?" Daryl asked. He was teasing us.

"It's one of those stories where you can't really explain to other people why it was interesting, but it was just a very intense time in my life."

"I had totally forgotten about that boy," Jill said.

It was almost eleven when we left. The restaurant had started to shut down, they turned a guy away at the door. I tried to pay the bill but Jill wouldn't let me; she wouldn't even let me pay my share. "Don't be the big-shot lawyer," she said. "This is my town, this is my treat."

In the parking lot afterward I said goodbye to people as if I might see them again. Daryl gave me his card. It took Jill a minute to find her keys; she had one of those tiny purses, which was basically just one pocket.

"Are you all right to drive?"

"I'm fine." Then we got in the car and she said, "I can't go to bed with you tonight. I don't know what you're expecting."

"That's fine, of course."

"I want to but I can't."

She pulled out of the strip-mall parking lot and we were back on one of those six-lane roads. Even late at night there was a constant flow of traffic. "Aren't you going to say anything?" she asked.

"What do you want me to say?"

"I don't know, something. Do you have any feelings about any of this?"

"I don't know, Jill. It's been a long day . . . I've been on the road since Saturday."

"Is that your reaction?"

"Why are you mad at me?"

"I forgot what you're like," she said. "You don't really care about anything."

For a few minutes I didn't answer. She stopped at a traffic light, then turned onto another highway. I was trying to explain myself in my head, but that meant when I opened my mouth, it came out over-rehearsed.

"I used to tell my kids, you don't have to do anything you'll regret. Most of the time you know beforehand, so you don't have to do it. So this . . . just seems like an example of that."

"Okay," she said.

"It's just something I used to tell them. I have this feeling like, I want to get through unscathed. Does that make sense?"

"Get through what?"

"I don't know. The next twenty years, the next two months, whatever it is."

"That sounds like a dumb way to live," she said.

"I don't want to leave behind me any messes for them to deal with that I couldn't deal with myself."

"You're making too big a deal out of all this, but whatever."

We were driving through her neighborhood now and then she pulled over outside her house instead of going up the driveway. She turned off the engine and we sat there. I didn't think it was my decision when to get out. Eventually she said, "I have a nice life, okay? I make good money, I try to help people. I get Friday afternoons off, so I can pick Katie up from school."

"You've got a great life."

"I don't want you to get the impression . . . I'm sorry, ignore me. I'm sorry I lost my temper. It just seemed really normal tonight, that's all."

"Me too," I said.

Then she turned on the car again and drove it under the car port. When we got inside she had to pay the babysitter. These interactions always take longer than you want them to but at least I didn't have to get involved. The house was quiet; they spoke in undertones. After Vanessa left, Jill said, "Let me just make up your bed."

"I can do it."

But of course she did it anyway; she pulled out the sofa bed, she got the sheets, she lowered the blinds. "Do you need anything else?" she said, then brought me a towel. "You know where the bathroom is. Don't worry about Katie. She sleeps through everything."

I couldn't fall asleep at first and then I woke up at 3 a.m. after a wet dream. I don't even remember what it was, it was just one of those stupid dreams. But I lay there for a few minutes in wet underwear trying not to let them touch the sheets. Eventually I had to get up and use the bathroom and felt the whole house creaking around me. Both bedrooms ran off the living room. I could have done without this, I thought, pissing into the pot, trying to avoid the water at the bottom, because the porcelain was quieter. By this I meant the whole thing, other people, puberty, middle age. Then I used my phone light to dig out a spare pair of Hanes from my backpack. I didn't want to wake up naked with a twelve-year-old girl in the house, but they were my last clean pair.

In the morning, I had to ask Jill to let me do a load of laundry. But she insisted on doing it herself, so I gave her all my clothes, wrapped up in a dirty T-shirt. She couldn't believe how swollen my face was, like a sponge leaking at the eyes.

"I'm taking you to a hospital right now."

"It's like this every morning. Then it goes down again. By lunchtime I look almost human."

"You need to see a doctor," she said. But I don't think she had the energy anymore to deal with me.

Katie had a soccer game at eleven but she didn't get up for breakfast. I ate a bowl of cereal in the kitchen, while Jill sat there, drinking coffee. She was planning to make pancakes later. I told her, "I'll get out of your hair, I need to hit the road."

"Where are you going now?"

She wasn't wearing makeup; I never thought of her as someone who wore a lot but I guess she did. She looked quite different, not just older, though she looked older, too.

"LA. I'm supposed to talk to this guy this afternoon. Michael can put me up."

"It's funny I've never met your kids."

"You never met Amy either."

"No."

"You'd probably like each other more than either of you likes me."

"Probably," she said.

When I left, she called out to Katie, "Come out and say goodbye to Uncle Tom." And Katie eventually came out in her pyjamas. "Who's Uncle Tom," she said.

"Don't be a smart-ass."

"Goodbye," she said, waving at me from her bedroom door.

III

I hadn't driven through Death Valley since Brian lived in LA. That was thirty years ago, the summer after we graduated. Jill was helping out at her mother's restaurant in Holbrook and I used to bounce between them, if a day's drive counts as bouncing—leaving one of them after breakfast and arriving in time for dinner with the other. I remembered a long empty nowhere in between, flat and horizonless, which worried me now, because the Volvo had done a lot of miles and one of the many male-oriented tasks I'm not particularly good at is taking care of my car. But in fact the road was fairly busy. Parts of it were under construction, with big vehicles parked beside the highway, and guys standing around in orange jackets in the dust. I spent an hour going five miles, lifting my foot off the brake to inch along, then braking again. So even if the car died somebody would probably stop to help. But the car was fine.

The dashboard temperature reached a hundred and nine. The air-conditioning didn't work when the car wasn't moving. I drank a lot of warm Dr Pepper.

On the long road, parts of my dream came back to me. When Amy told me about Zach, for three months we didn't touch each other in bed. It was like bunking in a youth hostel where you have to share a room with a member of the opposite sex. One night I woke up with an erection; Amy noticed and decided to relieve me. Without saying anything, she reached down, using one of my old T-shirts, which is what she slept in. This happened several times in the next few weeks. For some reason we didn't talk about it during the day. But for me it was both . . . shameful, because I let it happen and wanted it to happen, and erotically charged. I never knew if she would do it, I just lay there waiting. Eventually, to put a stop to this shameful period of our marriage, when she touched me I started kissing her and we made love in the normal way, like a husband and wife. But the dream I had at Jill's house was the other one, where I just lay there.

I thought about other things, too. I was beginning to feel pretty dislocated in time. That whole summer after college, driving between Jill and Brian, I had no idea what would happen next and was still caught up in both of these relationships. It must have seemed obvious that what mattered to me then would continue to shape my life. But of course neither Brian nor Jill played any real part in my next thirty years, and literally while you think these thoughts and have these feelings there's nothing around you except scrubland and other cars.

At last the foothills of . . . I don't want to say civilization but the suburbs of Los Angeles appeared. I was supposed to meet Todd at UCLA—a lot of NBA guys play pickup there in the offseason. Parking was tricky but I found a garage next to a Target, then wandered out into the afternoon sunshine looking for the gym. It felt good to stretch my legs. Santa Monica was about twenty degrees cooler than Las Vegas. Todd had said he'd leave my name at the desk, which in fact he had. I told the receptionist I was his lawyer.

Whenever I walk into a gym where basketball is being played, my heart rate ticks up. Just the echoes of those bouncing balls . . . It's not excitement exactly, more like nerves or fear, at the thought of having to stand up for myself against all those guys. There were several courts side by side and games going on in all of them, of various quality. The first face I recognized was Draymond Green's, then a few others fell into place. It took me a minute to find Todd. All I'd seen was his headshot on basketball-reference.com and a few YouTube highlights, mostly from his Wisconsin days. My impression was, he had a live body but didn't know what to do with it. He ran around a lot, he talked a lot, people ignored him. If he wanted the ball, he needed to get rebounds, which he was good at. Once I saw him jump over Draymond for a putback jam. But he also airballed a three and got his pocket picked trying to post up.

He wore a gray T-shirt that said PROVE ME WRONG on the back. The front said KOBE WAS A RAPIST in bright red letters. I didn't want to be there. What are you doing here . . . but it was just another thing I had to get through.

When his team lost, I introduced myself to Todd on the sidelines. Then he hit the showers and I waited outside on the campus lawn for him to come out. I was supposed to have dinner with Michael and some of his friends, after dropping my stuff at his apartment in Silver Lake. But it was almost six o'clock, so I called him and we had a short conversation. They were meeting at a place in Koreatown; maybe it was simpler for me to go straight there. I said to Michael, "I had Asian food last night." And he said, "What?"

"Japanese, in Las Vegas. Don't worry about it, it doesn't matter."

He said, "Korean is a totally different cuisine. I'll send you the link."

Todd came out, wet-haired and bouncy, carrying his gym bag over his shoulder, so I hung up. "Where do you want to go," I asked, and he said, "How about Rocco's?" So that's where we went; it was about a fifteen-minute walk, down Westwood Plaza.

There was a bar inside with red-leather bar stools and several TV screens hanging from the ceiling in all directions. On a Saturday evening in September they all showed college football. He ordered a Cherry Coke ("I don't drink alcohol," he said) and I had a club soda, and for the next hour and a half I listened to him talk.

His photograph made him seem better-looking than he was. Somehow in person the proportions were wrong. He was too tall, his shoulders were too narrow, his face looked small. When I found him annoying, I told myself, he's a twenty-three-year-old kid. In high school, he said, the black guys on the team wouldn't let him use the showers. They never actually beat him up but they made it clear. "I was a physically different person in those days; I weighed one-sixty-five. That's one of the reasons I started hitting the gym." In health class, they used to do stuff like leave a stick of Old Spice on his desk. His health teacher was the basketball coach. He just said, Todd doesn't smell that bad, leave him alone, stuff like that.

Todd said "stuff" a lot, he called the other kids "bozos" (like, those bozos); his vocabulary was strangely old-fashioned. "What bugged them was, I was a better athlete than them. I won every suicide, I could get my elbow to the rim."

At Wisconsin, things got better. Over half of the team was white. "Coach Sherman is all about the system," Todd said. "Everybody has his role to play. You can't just goof around. Most of the blue-chip black recruits don't want to be told what to do, especially not by a white head coach. They all want to run the show, even as freshmen. They want to get in their bags. But if you play for Coach Sherman, you're a part of something bigger than yourself, you have to sacrifice those individual talents for the greater good. That only appeals to a certain kind of player."

After working out all day, he was hungry and ordered a spaghetti marinara and then, when he finished that, another. I had a Sam Adams. I figured, if you have to listen to this stuff, you need a drink.

At the draft combine he had the fifth-highest standing vertical, 35½ inches. The four guys ahead of him were all

183

first-rounders. The Pistons didn't take him until the fifty-fifth pick. "You know what they made me do in training camp?" he said. "They gave me Earring Magic Ken to carry around. Do you know what that is? The gay Barbie. Because they think every good-looking white guy is gay."

"I thought all rookies had to do stupid shit."

"They opened up a Grindr account in my name and used to post secret pictures of me with my shirt off. Just because I have a good body and don't mind showing it, it's like, you must be gay."

"Who is they?" I said.

"Black guys on the team."

"How do you know they were black?"

"Because everyone else was black. You don't understand these guys, they look out for their own . . . but that's cool, if that's how they want to play it. We can play that game too."

"Who's we?"

"Come on, man. If you don't know who we is, I don't think I can explain it to you. Have you ever heard of Nietzsche?"

For a minute I didn't answer, but he just stared at me, waiting. "I've heard of him."

"He has this idea that he calls slave morality, which is basically the idea that, people, you know, to make themselves feel better, believe in all kinds of things that actually get in the way of who they are. Like equality. On the other side, you've got master morality, where for certain people you learn to accept your superiority and not be ashamed of it. But that's very hard to do if you're white in America right now."

"You understand that what you're saying . . ."

"That's the irony of it. We've all internalized slave morality, to the point where, we don't even want to accept our own superiority anymore. We're embarrassed by it, so we pretend it doesn't exist."

"You really think that's why there aren't more white basketball players?"

My phone rang; it was Michael calling. They couldn't get a table at Soban so we were going to Dan Sung Sa instead. "Okay," I said. "Just tell me where it is."

"How's it going?" he asked.

"I'll tell you later."

"There are a lot of great white basketball players right now," Todd said, "but they all come from Europe. You know who the last white American all-star was? Brad Miller, twenty years ago. Explain that to me. If there isn't something going on that's a lot bigger than Todd Gimmell. Do you know how many white Americans play in the NBA right now? Of the five hundred guys under contract, less than forty. You know what their average salary is? About six million dollars a year. You know what the league average is? Ten million. In any other business, this would be a lawsuit waiting to happen."

"Maybe white guys just aren't as good."

"How can you say that when the two best players in the world right now are white—Dončić and Jokić. From Slovenia and Serbia, with a combined population of nine million people. And neither one can jump over a phone book. Listen to me, Mr. Layward." (This was what he called me.) "If after everything I've told you, you still don't think there's a whole culture of systematic discrimination against white American basketball players, then, as my dad likes to say, I've got a bridge to sell you."

"I don't understand who you want to sue. America? For discriminating against white men?"

"Let's just start with the NBA, okay? You know what my nickname was at the Denver Nuggets? The Accountant. You know why? Because I'm white, that's why."

"Who called you that?"

"The Nuggets play-by-play guy, Howard Love. But the team used it in their promotional material. Imagine calling a black guy The Drug Dealer. It's the same thing."

"I don't think it's the same thing."

But what else was I supposed to say? When you talk to crazy people, they're all expert in their particular branch of craziness. So you can't win these arguments, you just have to let them talk. But the whole time I was conscious we were in a student bar, and Todd was not somebody who modulated his voice. I also heard, in the back of my head, Miri saying to me, Angry White Male. Angry white male angry white male . . . this is the road you're going down, this is where it leads you.

So I said, "Listen Todd, I've got to . . . I'm supposed to meet my son for dinner."

"I'm sorry, Mr. Layward. I've been chewing your ear off. Can I call you next week? I'm still in the process of putting together a list of names. A lot of guys don't want to talk about what's going on, because they still have to play in this league, and the rest are in the media. They can't afford to stick their necks out. But I'll be in touch," he said.

I paid the bill. He was eating when I left, hunched over the wooden bar with a gym bag at his feet. The whole time we were there, nobody asked for his autograph. He could still live a normal life and looked like any other student, except taller.

It was still light outside, which surprised me. About eighty degrees, without the air-conditioning. My car was parked a few blocks away.

At the restaurant, Michael and his friends were already sitting down at a long wooden bar. I was the last to arrive. Red banners hung from the ceiling, the smell of chilies caught in my throat. My son had saved a chair next to him but he stood up to give me a hug before introducing me. I held him longer than he wanted me to. But it was too loud to really talk, there were too many people. For the last two years, my dinner companions had been Miri and Amy and nobody else; and now I was going out every night in large groups.

On my right-hand side was a pretty girl. Girl is wrong, I couldn't tell how old she was. Michael had deliberately put me between the two of them, but I couldn't talk to both at once. I had to turn one way or the other.

"I'm sorry," I said, "I didn't catch your name."

So she spelled it out for me: B-E-T-J-E. "It's Dutch," she said. "People call me Betcha, but that's not how you say it, so I tell them to call me Betty."

"What does Michael call you?"

"I haven't figured that out yet."

"Are you the vet?" I asked.

Sitting down, she had quite a tall person's presence—and like a movie star, a head that seemed just a little too big for her body. But she was very pretty. After the meal, when she stood up, I realized she was only about five-two.

"Who told you that?"

"My daughter. Michael told her you have a hinterland."

"I wonder what he means by that," she said.

"I think he means anybody who ever had a real job."

"What?" she said.

"Somebody who had a job."

There was a time-lag in the conversation, because of the noise. You had to repeat yourself, but it meant people sometimes followed their own train of thought.

"I was a vet but didn't like it. I just liked animals but didn't want to cut them up. A lot of what you end up doing is not really necessary, but you have to do it if you want to make money. The whole business is paid for by insurance. Anyway, I quit. It was just one of those ideas you have as a girl, about what you want to do with your life; in my case, I let it go on too long."

She used to live in Twin Bridges, Montana. Which was

another one of those ideas . . . She worked for this practice off Route 287. There were mountains all around, there were wheat fields, but there weren't a lot of men. "Well, I had a bad experience. That's why I moved there, to have experiences. But I didn't like that much either."

"Maybe this is what he means by a hinterland."

"Eventually I decided, you need to get a little closer to where the action is. So I applied to grad school . . . in philosophy."

Later she said, "Michael thinks I'm something that I'm not."

We were having this conversation with him on the other side of me, but I don't think he could hear. I could barely hear her myself and had to lean over, with my elbow on the bar and my head down.

"What's that?"

"A serious person, at least, that's what he wants me to be."

"What are you working on?"

"Non-human consciousness. But nobody's interested, all the money right now is in AI. But there's actually a lot of overlap."

I tried to ask her more but it was too loud. You couldn't have a technical discussion. And I wanted to talk to Michael, too; I was aware that he was very aware of our conversation. Meanwhile, the food kept coming, in small metal bowls. Chicken wings, grilled Spam, some kind of corn cheese. We drank a sparking rice wine, which tasted a little like hibiscus tea. He said, "How are you doing," and I said, "I'm very happy to be here, I'm happy to see you." And he said, "No, what are you doing here, why are you here."

"I don't know, Michael. I can't talk about it here, you have to shout."

"How long are you staying?"

"I don't know."

He looked at me, not reproachfully, but with his reserved-judgment face. It was easier to talk to Betty. There were about eight of us in a row, all of them philosophers. But I didn't really talk to anyone else. Afterward, somebody suggested karaoke. There was a place called Brass Monkey you could walk to. I said to Michael, "If it's possible, I'd like to go to bed. I've been on the road since breakfast, it's been a long day."

Betty wanted to go, though. So they had a complicated conversation. He said, "Are you going?" And she said, "That's the plan."

We were outside the restaurant now, standing on Sixth Street in the rough warm traffic-flavored evening air. It was easier to talk. Betty had on black leggings and Nike running shoes, with a neon yellow swoosh; she wore an oversized men's shirt.

"Do you want me to come too?" he asked.

"I thought your dad wanted to go to bed."

"I can give him the keys."

"You should see your dad."

"I'll see him in the morning . . . I'm just saying, if you want me to come too, I don't think he'd care."

"It's fine, I don't mind. There are a lot of people going."

"I want you to . . . I'd like you guys to spend some time."

"How long is he staying for?"

"I don't know, he doesn't know."

"Is he here tomorrow?"

"I'll be here tomorrow," I said.

"Do you want to go to the beach?"

"I was hoping to take Michael to see his grandfather's grave."

"Where's that?"

"Newport Beach. I don't know how far that is."

"About an hour away," Betty said. "What about tomorrow night?"

"I'm supposed to work tomorrow night." (Michael had a job at a restaurant in West Hollywood, which I didn't know about.)

"What time's your shift?"

"It starts at five."

"So we can hang out in the afternoon. Let's have lunch at Annenberg. We can go swimming afterward."

"I'm not sure my father wants to go swimming."

"I'm happy to do whatever you want to do."

"Great," Betty said. "It's a date." But she was saying it to both of us. They all walked off in a gang along Sixth Street, and Michael and I went to our separate cars.

It was a short drive to his apartment on Duane Street, opposite the dog park. There were a lot of apartment buildings around there, in various styles, but all of them fairly modern. Michael's looked like an ocean liner. I rang the buzzer and he let me in, and I walked up the concrete stairwell, carrying my backpack. Thinking, every night, you're sleeping somewhere new—not happily or sadly, but just because it was a fact.

"You're growing a beard," he said, when he opened the door.

"Well, I'm trying to make myself more resistible to women."

"How's that working out?"

"Not well."

"Ha ha," he said. "How long have you been saving that one up?"

"About three thousand miles. When I left the house, I didn't bring my shaving things. I didn't know how long I would be gone."

Michael had a second-floor unit, with a balcony overlooking Silver Lake Boulevard. I had never been to his place before. It was very simple, but he had Naftali taste; there was an old rug on the floor, and one of those Eames leather recliners in the window. He had made a bookcase out of bricks and boards, painted gray. But it was also the apartment of someone who lived alone and was slowly collecting a few nice things to carry with him to his next apartment.

It was after eleven; he offered me a drink, but I just wanted to go to bed. Michael insisted I take his room. He said he wanted to do a little work anyway.

"Where are you going to sleep?" I said.

"I've got a very expensive air mattress. But sometimes I sleep on the recliner anyway."

"Come on, Michael. I don't want to kick you out."

"It's fine, I really don't mind. But just . . . this can't be like a permanent arrangement."

"Of course not."

He let me use the bathroom first; I borrowed his toothpaste. "The sheets are clean," he said. "I changed them this morning." He gave me a towel and I washed my face.

"Thank you, son. By the way, I liked the look of Betty."

"Me too," he said. "But seriously, Dad . . . How long do you plan to be in town?"

"I've kind of gone beyond plans at the moment."

"Well, we can talk in the morning."

His bedroom was very tidy. (Even as a teenager he used to line up the pencils on his desk; you had to be careful if you touched anything, he always knew.) There was a ficus under the window, in a large terra-cotta pot, and a stack of *New Yorker*s on his bedside table. The mattress was on the hard side and it took me a while to fall asleep. I could see the light from the living room under the door, and later, much later, heard him talking quietly to someone on the phone. It was the . . . I don't know how to describe it, the sharpest taste I'd had in years of what it feels like to be young.

In the morning, when I came to breakfast, he said, "What happened to you?"

"It's fine, it goes away."

"How long has this been going on?"

"A few months. I told you . . . you saw me last week in New York."

"This is worse. When's the last time you went to the doctor?"

"Let me just get a cup of coffee before we have this conversation."

He had one of those fancy Italian machines, which was too complicated for me to work, so he had to make it. He said, "When's the last time you went to the doctor?"

"In May. That was when I first got symptoms."

"Remind me what he said."

"He said it's probably long Covid. I can refer you to a treatment program, but the truth is, for someone like you, who is basically functional, there's not much they can do."

"That's what we're doing this morning. I'm taking you to the emergency room."

"Just wait a couple of hours. It goes away."

"Did the doctor see you like this?"

By this point, I was drinking his coffee and eating a bowl of his Grape Nuts. He had one of those white tulip tables in the living room, which was big enough for two people. The light came in through the balcony windows; it was a nice place to sit.

"This is a more recent phenomenon. But . . . look, I'm happy to go the doctor, but I don't want to sit in the ER all day while my symptoms disappear. It's Sunday now, I can call Dr. Shulquist in the morning."

"But he's in New York."

"Of course he is."

"When are you going back to New York?"

"That's another conversation," I said.

In the end, he agreed to let me see a doctor in LA, once I worked out who was covered by my insurance. But today we were driving out to Newport Beach to see his grandfather's grave. That was what I wanted to do.

We took his car. It's a funny thing to be driven around by your son, you feel the power dynamic shifting. He had an old Acura Legend, which he'd bought secondhand and still smelled of cigarettes. But it was a nice-looking car and I thought, Betty wouldn't mind driving around in this. The air-conditioning stank though, at least at first, so he turned it on and kept the windows open until we got to the highway. After that the road was too loud.

At Long Beach, we hit the PCH. It was pleasant driving, there was always something to see—palm trees and beach-front condos and motels, donut shops and boats on the water and sprawling Chinese restaurants.

Michael asked me, "When's the last time you spoke to Mom?"

"Are you having the talk with me?" I was kidding around but he didn't respond, so I said, "About a week ago. When I called she kept hanging up on me, but then she stopped calling."

"I told her to give you a little space. What about Miri?"

"No. I wanted to leave her alone, I didn't want any of this to get in the way of her first week at school. Did you ever tell her about . . . what happened?"

"What happened?"

"Your mother's affair. I still don't know if she knows."

"I didn't think it was my business."

The car had a CD player, but it was broken. The only thing you could listen to was what was stuck inside, which was a Neil Young CD. Michael was sick of it but turned it on anyway. *Hello cowgirl in the sand . . . the damage done. Helpless helpless*, etc.

"Sometimes . . . don't mention this to her, by the way. She still uses our Spotify account, so I check in on what she's listening to."

"What's she listening to?"

"A lot of Elvis. The Womack Sisters, whoever they are. There was a break-up song, which made me think, maybe she's having a hard time. But maybe it's just a song."

"How do you know it was a break-up song?"

"That's what it was called. I didn't listen to it. If I listen to it, Spotify switches to my device."

"I talked to her yesterday. She's fine."

"Did you tell her I was coming?" It was easier for him not to talk, because he was driving, so I had to repeat myself.

"Of course," he said.

"What did you say?"

"Look, she knows you guys are going through . . . some heavy weather. I don't think that's news to anyone."

All of this makes it look like we were having a conversation, but it was more like, sometimes one of us spoke. We had reached the outskirts of Newport Beach and passed the hospital where my father died. Then we crossed over the water and turned inland, we were driving through suburban southern California.

"Your mother sent me a somewhat cryptic email, with a link to a listing for an apartment on the Upper East Side."

"I think that was meant for me."

"Does she send you a lot of those?"

"Sometimes," he said.

"What's she looking for, somewhere . . . just for her or . . . what's the idea."

"Why don't you ask her?"

"We're not really communicating right now."

But then we arrived. There was a parking lot just inside the entrance. All of the roads were smoothly surfaced, the grass made it look like a golf course. There was even a low, arched building that might have been the club house or a Ramada Inn.

Michael said, "Do we park and walk, or what do we do?"

"I don't know. It's a pretty big place. Let's stay in the car."

So we drove around for a while. What I didn't realize, most of the graves were just set into the grass, lying down, like stepping stones. But there were also concrete monuments, inlaid with brass plaques, and other strange architectural features . . . squares of walled-off garden with their own benches, and pillared cloisters with names like

Sunset Court carved into the stone. I had emailed the mortuary a few days ago to ask directions, and someone had sent me a map. But I'm not very good with maps. Michael pulled over and we stared at my phone together.

"Where are we now?" he said.

"I don't know."

"Aren't there street names?"

So I got out to look. It was another perfect September day, the skies were as blue and well-kept as the grass was green. In the distance, beyond the low hills of the cemetery, you could see the residential tree canopy of Newport Beach, with white houses scattered in between, and a handful of high-rises downtown.

"I think Sunset Court is the name of the street," I said.

It took us half an hour to find him. My father had one of the stones laid in the grass. Some yellow flowers in a pot stood next to his grave. I reached down to touch them; they were real. The inscription read:

John Layward

1943–2020

He is gone into the world of light.

We stood looking at it for a minute. I don't know what you're supposed to get from these things but I waited to receive it.

Eventually Michael said, "*Is* gone?"

"*Has* gone?"

"I don't know. I didn't know he was religious."

"He wasn't."

"So why . . ."

"I guess he was in no position to object."

But I thought, did he get through the second half of his life without making himself particularly well-known or had he just given up on certain opinions? Like his hatred of religion; maybe it turned out that was only important to him in the context of his battle with my mother. With another woman, he was perfectly willing to go along with things.

I said, "Kobe Bryant is buried here too."

"Okay . . ."

"Do you want to see it?"

"Sure. Why not."

So we drove around looking for his grave. It was easier to talk to him in the car, I didn't have to look at him. The speed limit was ten miles an hour. I opened my window and he turned off the air-conditioning.

"I don't want you to think, Michael, that I don't think about things from your mother's point of view. I try to. I'm also trying to figure out why I reacted to what happened the way I did. I mean, how much was moral indignation or . . . disappointment, and how much was just wounded sexual vanity."

"Am I really the person you should have this conversation with?"

"I thought you were a moral philosopher." Then I said, "I need to talk to someone. I don't know who to talk to."

"I want to be helpful to you, Dad. But I don't think this is a conversation where I can be objective."

"Okay. I'm sorry."

We couldn't find his grave. Later I read a story in the *New York Post* that said people had mistaken someone else's gravesite for Kobe's, and the cemetery had to issue a public statement, because so many people were coming to see the wrong grave. They had to increase security, everyone left flowers. I should have brought something to my father's grave. But the lawn was so clean, and everything so well-tended, that I wouldn't have wanted to leave an obvious mark—something his other children could see.

On the drive back into LA, I talked about Todd Gimmell, because of the T-shirt. Michael said he was surprised the other guys didn't beat him up. I said their attitude seemed to be bored toleration. He said, sometimes that's the best you can hope for. He asked me if I planned on pursuing that particular line of interest, and I told him, no, that's all over. I'm not going back to the law school either, I'm done with all that. I don't want to fight these fights anymore. I need to think of something else to do with the rest of my life.

We were late for lunch with Betty. There was an accident outside Inglewood and we sat in traffic for half an hour. Michael asked me to text Betty from his phone, so I pretended to be Michael and said, "Sorry stuck in traffic with my dad, he made us drive around looking for Kobe's grave." Which was true, but it upset Michael when I told him. He said, "That's not how I talk about you to other people," so I apologized.

It was after two when we pulled into the Annenberg Center and parked; Betty had a table outside, in the sand. She didn't seem to mind.

My father took me to the beach the first time we came to LA, after the divorce. Eric was supposed to come too, but he got food poisoning on the plane and stayed in his room. Our stepmother was something of a hypochondriac, at least that's how I remember her. But I guess she was also a thirty-year-old woman who had recently split up a marriage and was trying to have her first baby. When Eric started throwing up she refused to go near him. They had a two-bedroom apartment, but the second bedroom was really just a glorified closet; it had no windows. That's where Eric and I slept.

I told this story at lunch. The food was actually pretty good. I had a Santa Fe salad, with beans and guacamole. Betty had the vegan burger and let me take a bite—it tasted like a burger.

Michael said, "I haven't heard that story before."

"Which beach?" Betty asked.

"I don't remember. They were living in Culver City, before moving to Newport Beach after the baby was born. But we never came back, Eric refused to go. It was not a successful visit. And I don't think she wanted us, after the baby."

"What about you, did you want to go?"

She wore a wraparound dress over her bikini, something floaty. But her body or physical presence was strangely formal. She sat very straight in her chair, and the breeze kept blowing her dress across the table.

"It wasn't really an option at the time. I mean, expressing an opinion. Mom was just barely hanging on."

"But you wanted to go."

"You have to understand . . . my mother was the voice of fear in our household; my father was the voice of indifference. As a teenage kid, I preferred indifference. My brother's a lot younger, he still wanted to be coddled. Later, when I went to Pomona, I thought I might get to see my dad a bit more. Which I suppose I did, to some extent. But he already had another life. It wasn't easy for him." Nobody else said anything, so I kept going. "When he took me to the beach . . . afterward he said, that's your first taste of the Pacific. For some reason I remember that. It's nice of you to let me talk so much."

"Dad," Michael said.

It was almost four o'clock when we finished eating; the heat of the day, but you could already feel the light beginning to change.

"Are we swimming?" Betty said. "Come on, I've been sitting in these silly clothes all afternoon."

"I'm not swimming, I have to go to work in an hour."

I said to Betty, "I don't have any trunks. We didn't have a chance to go home before coming here."

But they sold swimsuits at the café, along with other beach things, buckets and shovels and goggles and towels. I was worried that the same thing might happen to me that happened in Jill's pool, but I also didn't want to say no to what it seemed like the day had to offer. So I bought a pair and got changed in one of the bathrooms outside. There were outdoor showers, too. Betty said I could share her towel, and we walked across the hot sand to the water.

Michael wore Saucony running shoes and a polo shirt. He had shaved that morning and his face looked sensitive in the sun, scraped thin. Betty gave him her dress and purse and he sat a little awkwardly on her towel, while she ran into the water.

Even when she ran she moved with a certain stiffness of deliberation or self-consciousness. She had short legs and a long upper body. I rolled up the rest of my clothes in my jeans and gave them to Michael too, then walked slowly into the ocean. The water felt very cold. I thought, so long as you stay upright, you'll probably be fine. But standing waist-deep in the surf, I just got colder and colder, so when a wave came rolling in, I jumped against it and came out the other side. I could feel the salt in my eyes, in the sun. It had taken me three thousand miles to get here, but I was here. Maybe this was what my father felt. Betty was already twenty feet out and calling something to Michael that I couldn't hear. I swam hard to warm up and felt the pressure on my face building and building. Then another wave came and I jumped in again. If you don't go near her, she won't notice.

You forget how much fun it is just to wait for a big wave . . . When the kids were small they could spend hours like this. Even as teenagers, when we took them to the Cape, they reverted. It's enough to think about, just trying to get the timing right, so when a wave starts cresting, you begin to crawl ahead of it toward shore, hoping to carry its momentum with you. Then afterward it spits you onto the beach. I could feel the sand in my new shorts.

Betty started swimming beside me, while Michael watched. Then he stood up and came to the edge of the water.

"Dad," he said. "We gotta go. I've got to get to work."

"What do you . . ."

"I can drive him home," Betty said. She was sitting in the water now, with her legs stretched out; about two feet deep, letting the waves swing her around. I was aware of other people up and down the beach, but the breeze was strong enough that you felt like, a little pocket of privacy around you in the wind.

"You don't have to do that."

"It's fine."

"I think you should come in," Michael said. "You're turning blue."

"It's just too cold to stand around."

"So let's go."

"Can you get me the towel?" Betty asked, and the afternoon was over. She wrapped it around her while she was still in the water; then they walked up the beach together to the piles of clothes. I waited for her to get dressed and tried to stand as still as possible to let the sun warm me up.

"Are you all right?" Betty said.

"I've got . . . middle-aged circulation. I just get cold."

"I'm sorry it's wet," she said, giving me the towel. She

looked cold too, under the thin dress; there were goosebumps on her arms and her cheeks had gone red in the wind.

But it was warmer up the beach. I still had to shower and get dressed and Michael kept looking at his watch. Betty said, "Don't be stupid, I can drive him back."

I left them to argue it out and wandered over to the outdoor shower, but it was broken. At least, I couldn't get any pressure; I kept hitting the knob but it only squirted at me. Then in the bathroom I almost fell over. I was bending down to pull on my shoes (the Converse are always tricky) and felt the flush coming back to my face and a noise in my ears like a fly dying against an electric heater. For a minute I put my hand against the door and waited for the darkness to pass, before tying the laces.

Michael called out, "Dad, look, I've really got to go."

Then I opened the door and went out.

"You don't look well," Betty said.

"Let me at least drive you to the car." It turned out that Betty had walked to the beach. She was house-sitting for one of her professors, who was spending the semester at the American Academy in Berlin. Michael said, "This is what she's like, you think you're talking to a hick from Montana and it turns out that she's friends with Steven Pinker."

"I actually grew up in Seattle. But whatever."

"I'm happy to walk," I said. "It'll give me a chance to warm up."

"Are you all right?" Michael asked.

"I'm fine."

"I'm sorry I have to do this."

We were in the parking lot, next to his car. Just hanging around, he didn't want to leave. Then Betty and I watched him drive away, and I felt the slight awkwardness of our situation.

"I don't know why he has this job," Betty said, to break the silence.

"He doesn't want to be dependent on me in any way."

"That's Michael," she said.

We had to walk up the steep stairs cut into the hillside to reach the top of the Palisades. I felt strangely out of breath. I even said to Betty, "I'm sorry, just give me a minute," and sat down on one of the benches in the park. Behind us the ocean stretched out flat and glittery, around us the palm trees cast thin shadows in the grass.

"That's fine, take as long as you want."

She was waiting, she was being patient, and I felt like, the old man.

"All right, let's go."

It's a beautiful walk, along Ocean Avenue and then up Adelaide, with the canyon at your feet and all the millionaires' houses among the trees and the whole landscape draining below you to the beach. Michael had mentioned to me that Betty hoped to get a job with the CIIS, which was a sort of pseudo-philosophical institute founded in the sixties and devoted to the study of consciousness. Part of its mission was to train healers. Michael was fairly suspicious of their claims, so when I asked about it, Betty laughed.

"What did he say," she said. "Tell me what he said."

"He said it was in San Francisco."

"You're lying," she said.

"It's not in San Francisco?"

"Don't be a jerk."

But she also talked more seriously about it. One of the reasons she'd wanted to be a vet was because she was very interested . . . in healing, I don't know how to put it without sounding corny. But healing just seems like a very interesting process. It means such different things in different contexts. Like, is the idea of healing to get you back to the way you used to be or to turn you into something new? That seems like a pretty significant difference, even at the biological level, but Michael thinks . . . whenever people talk about something that doesn't have a very concrete meaning, he gets uncomfortable. He thinks they're trying to scam him. Just because some things that are real are also hard to pin down. I'm sorry, I'm not explaining myself very well.

"No, no, I know what you mean."

When we got to her house, she said, "Do you want to come in? I can make tea."

"That might be nice; I still feel a little cold."

It was one of those American neighborhoods where you think, how can anyone be unhappy here? With so much money, and such wide streets, and such carefully maintained lawns. Betty's professor lived in a 1930s house with dark wooden floors and a grand piano in the front window. There was an extension at the back, which you reached through a narrow stairway, and that's where Betty was staying. It had its own kitchen and a balcony overlooking the pool. She put the kettle on and brought out some pecan brittle, which she said was all she had to eat.

"I don't know how old it is."

But I snapped off a bit; I thought the sugar might do me good. There was a table on the balcony, where we sat; but the room was basically her bedroom. Her bed was made and had a Hudson's Bay blanket lying across it.

"You still look blue," she said.

"Maybe I could take a shower? The one at the beach was broken. I wouldn't mind getting the salt off."

"There's only a bathtub." But she showed me the way and gave me a fresh towel. Then I closed the door behind me. What are you doing, I thought. Why are you here. But even the flow of hot water into the tub felt good; the bathroom began to steam up. And I took off my clothes and got in and let the water fill up around me. Even when I was walking up the hill I felt a kind of shivering in my core that I couldn't control.

I don't know how long I lay there, with my eyes closed. I almost fell asleep.

But when I got out again I felt very very strange. Maybe I stood up too quickly. It was as if something in my blood had begun to effervesce, and it was bubbling up inside me, in my chest. My face felt flushed and hot. I called out, "Betty?" and eventually she said, "Is everything all right?"

I managed to put the towel around me before opening the door. "I think I need to lie down."

"He's naked, I don't want to touch him." I could hear her talking on the phone. "Of course I did. I don't know. Just before I called you. I don't *know*."

I was lying on the woolen blanket, which felt scratchy against my legs. I could have opened my eyes but didn't want to, so I just lay there.

Michael arrived before the ambulance. He had time to help me get dressed and brought my clothes in from the bathroom. They were still damp, and I could feel the sand and salt in the jeans and socks and underwear. To put on my shoes, I lay back on the bed and pulled. Betty retreated into the kitchen and Michael went to say something to her. They had a private conversation, the only thing I could hear was the tone. Then the doorbell rang.

The paramedics brought a stretcher with them. I said, "I'm fine, I'm okay," but Michael insisted. The trouble was the narrow stairway. I actually had to get off the stretcher while they carried it down and then walk down the stairs myself, with Michael carefully preceding me. Afterward, they made me get back on.

"This is foolishness," I said to Michael.

"What do you expect when you passed out."

"I fell asleep," I said. But okay. So I let them carry me to the ambulance. Betty came out into the front yard, looking small. She said to Michael, "Call me, let me know what's going on," as we left. And I felt . . . many things. Glad that they had this kind of a relationship, where trouble for one was trouble for both. But I had also reached the age where I was the trouble.

In the ambulance, I wanted to sit up, but they kept me on the stretcher. Somebody took my blood pressure, they took my pulse. Both were on the high side. They asked me, how do you feel? Do you have any chest pain? No. Any breathlessness? Not right now. But earlier? Well, I'd been swimming, we were walking up from the beach. Any other symptoms? My hands are cold. Even now? Yes, but that's normal for me. I often have cold hands. But when I looked at them, the knuckles were swollen and red. The skin was dry. When I was a kid I remember being fascinated by my grandmother's hands (my father's mother), in a horrified way—I didn't want to eat anything she cooked, I didn't want her to touch me. This was what my hands were like.

It was only a ten-minute drive; I could see the flash of the siren out of the darkened back windows. Michael sat next to me. His face was Amy's face in the half-light; his face was Amy's face.

"What happened back there?" he said.

"I don't know. I just woke up like that. I didn't do anything wrong."

"That's not what I meant."

"I just felt funny coming out of the bath. What did she tell you?"

"That's what she said. You passed out."

When we parked, he took my hand and then let go, so they could carry me inside.

It was like going through a time warp into an earlier phase of the pandemic. Everyone wore masks. Michael picked up a couple from the reception desk; the one in the back of my jeans was old and dirty. After that there was a lot of waiting around; I had to fill out paperwork for the insurance. They wheeled me into a private room and one of the nurses gave me an ECG, for which she had to take off my shirt. I felt a little ashamed of the state of my body, the veins on my stomach and the purple network of bruises under my heart. With my shirt on, I looked like a healthy middle-aged man. But the ECG was fine, I hadn't had a heart attack. She carefully removed all the adhesive nodes, trying not to tear out my chest hair. "This is fun," I said to her, through the soft artificial material. "Some people pay a lot of money for this."

"I know, right," she said. But she had other things to do.

They left us alone for a while. Michael took out his phone and said, "I want you to tell me all your symptoms, from the beginning." So I went over everything: sudden exhaustion, irregular heartbeat, the bruising, bloating in the morning, leaky eyes, circulation trouble, protruding veins, head rushes every time I stand up, a feeling of pressure on my face . . . He wrote it all down on his phone. Then he started googling.

"I don't think that's helpful," I said.

"You want to think of these people as the experts and put yourself in their hands and abdicate responsibility. But all the studies show that the way you tell your story plays a big part in the diagnosis."

"Where do you get this stuff," I said.

"This is one of the things that Betty writes about."

They had transferred me to a narrow hospital bed, with a hard mattress and a roll of paper stretched across it. I needed to take a leak but Michael didn't want to let me walk unassisted. "This foolishness has gone on long enough," I said and stood up. Then wandered out looking for a bathroom; Michael let me go. When I came back he was still staring at his phone. I sat on the bed and lay down. You could see my shoe prints on the crumpled paper.

"Is there any water in here?"

"Do you want some water?"

"I wouldn't mind a drink. But I'm happy to get it myself."

So he went out to find some water and came back a few minutes later with a paper cup. I had to scooch, to sit up in the bed. I was starting to feel more normal, a little more like myself; it helped to sit up. The pressure on my chest and face was receding.

"It's funny, she doesn't seem older than you."

Eventually he said, "Why should she seem older?"

"Isn't she older?"

"About six years."

"That's not nothing. At your age. Except in the way she moves," I said.

He didn't answer at first. I couldn't tell if he was annoyed.

"She had a car accident in high school, she's had a lot of back surgery. She's a much more fragile person than she appears."

"I can believe it," I said.

A little later the doctor came in. Her name was Dr. Kalra;

she looked mid-thirties, she seemed basically to be a very worried person. I liked her, though, she took her time. She asked me what happened, and I told her. I passed out coming out of the bath; maybe I fell asleep. Michael said, "He was unconscious for about a minute."

"Were you there?"

"No . . . according to a friend of mine."

"Is this the first time this has happened?"

"I don't know, maybe. A few months ago, I got up in the night to take a leak and fell down; it was just a head rush. It wasn't a big deal. I get a lot of head rushes."

"Is there anything else?"

So I told her my other symptoms; I lifted my shirt and showed her the veins and bruises. She asked me to take it off and put a stethoscope to my chest. Breathe in, breathe out, the usual routine. She said, "Are you comfortable standing up?" And I said, "Sure." So I stood up, and she told me to lift my arms above my head. Breathe in, breathe out; the mask felt hot against my face.

"All right," she said. "You can get dressed."

Then she went out. There was a door to another room, and I could hear her talking, and another voice, a man's, responding. She didn't sound happy. I could hear her saying, "I think you should look at him," but then, a minute later, she came back in.

Michael said, "What do you think it is?"

"There's clearly an obstruction somewhere. I'd like to do a CT scan."

"He thinks it's long Covid."

"I don't think it's long Covid," she said.

"Does it have to be tonight? I'm a little hungry."

"There's a cafeteria downstairs. You're welcome to get some food."

"We'll get the scan tonight," Michael told her.

She sent us to another part of the hospital, where we sat in an ordinary waiting room, on the hard plastic chairs with everybody else; this time I was allowed to walk. Eventually they called my name, and Michael asked, "Do you want me to go with you?"

"I'm all grown up," I said. "I'll be fine."

But then as I went in, I felt a sugar rush of fear. This is where it starts. This is where it starts. I had to take off my clothes and put on one of those blue gowns, which you tie at the back. There was a cubbyhole for me to get changed in, with a lock; afterward, I carried around the key. The radiologist was a Brazilian guy, a very skinny guy with a gentle and not totally reassuring manner. His mask kept slipping under his nose. He may not have been the radiologist, maybe he was just a technician. It was his job to get the cannula in. But I hadn't had anything to drink in several hours, apart from that paper cup of water. He found a vein but it died on him, it stopped bleeding. I kept my eyes closed. He tried several times, then another technician came in. When she introduced herself, I looked down and saw a red mess of gauze and bandage taped loosely to the back of my wrist. So I shut my eyes again. But she made it work.

"It's flowing nicely now," she said. "Are you all right to walk?"

"I'm fine."

They sent me into another room, where the scanner was, one of those coffin-shaped capsules with a long tongue of bed reaching into the deep plastic mouth. Everything looked very expensive; everything looked very clean. It looked like, if you programmed it right, you could lie in that tube and teleport to another galaxy. Or just, anywhere else but here. The radiologist was another healthy stranger. Behind the masks these interactions felt more functional; your face remained a private space. He said, we'll give you a little injection, it's a contrast dye. You might feel like you have to go to the bathroom. That's normal.

"What do I do with this key?" I asked.

There was a hook for me to hang it on. Then I lay down on the moving bed and waited for it to slide me in.

The whole thing took about ten minutes, that's what they told me beforehand. So I tried to work out how long ten minutes is. You have to keep very still. Also, I was supposed to hold my arms over my head and that turned out to be difficult. The pins and needles began almost immediately. By the end my arms felt like rolled-up sailcloth, dead weights. Sometimes I had to breathe in and hold my breath, then let it out when they told me to. A voice spoke to me from the tube. But there were also periods of silence.

This is what I thought about. I tried to concentrate on specific things. Poems I had memorized in high school. The

Raven . . . Once upon a midnight dreary, until it broke down. Whose woods these are I think I know. Ozymandias. Nothing beside remains . . . Famous moments in sports from my childhood. Jordan switching to his left hand midair against the Lakers . . . Lorenzo Charles catching Derek Whittenburg's airball and dunking it home as time expired to win the 1983 National Championship. I imagined Jimmy Valvano running like a man released onto the court, looking for people to hug. A few years later he was dead of cancer. All of this added up to maybe six minutes' worth of material, then I went back to the beginning.

Then it was over; the bed I lay on quietly slid out of the tube.

"Just give me a moment," I said. "I'm not very good at standing up after I've been lying down."

Slowly the feeling returned into my arms.

It was almost midnight before we got back to Michael's apartment in Silver Lake. We had to wait to see Dr. Kalra again; she was waiting for the blood results. There was some mix-up at the lab. She didn't want to sign me out until she had them. But she said, this isn't a prison. We can't keep you here against your will. It was Michael I had to persuade. I said, just give me one more night of normal life. Please. I promise like a good boy I'll come back in the morning. We had to take a cab in the end; he'd left his car at Betty's house.

We were having breakfast when I got the call. I wanted to go jogging but Michael said, just take it easy, all right. I ran three days ago, do you really think something has changed in the last three days? You passed out yesterday, give yourself a day off. You can go running tomorrow. I didn't pass out, I fell asleep.

But I did as I was told and sat around in my boxer shorts eating cereal. My face was the way it always was after I woke up, bloated and featureless, something you want to hide from other people. Which was fine, I couldn't really see anyway, through watery eyes.

Everyone knows what the call is, where the phone rings and your life is different afterward. Some people probably get it more than once. A voice said, may I speak to Mr. Layward? And I said, speaking. His name was Dr. Liebman; he had a nice voice, he had the voice of a guy with small kids. Michael stood over me and I held the phone a little away from my ear so he could hear. I didn't want to hear this alone or have to explain it afterward. Dr. Liebman said he wanted to talk to me about the scan. I'm afraid I have some bad news. What it showed was a large tumor in your mediastinum; this explains why you've been having all these symptoms. I said, I don't know what the mediastinum is. It's a kind of pocket in your chest, between the heart and the lungs. A lot of blood vessels come together there, but you don't have any nerve endings, which is why you didn't feel anything.

"How large is large?" I asked.

"Well, there are different ways of measuring it. About six inches in diameter."

"The size of a fist."

"Maybe a little bigger than a fist. We think it's probably lymphoma. That's why I'm calling, and not Dr. Kalra. I'm part of the cancer team. The good news about lymphoma is that most of them respond well to treatment."

I'm paraphrasing what he said because it's hard to remember these things exactly. We talked for about half an hour. He wouldn't get off the phone until I finished asking him anything I wanted to ask him; Michael had a few questions too. He wanted to know what stage it was. That's hard to say, until we do another scan. But staging for lymphoma is a little different than it is for other cancers, what matters more is the kind of lymphoma you're dealing with rather than the spread. The next step is taking a biopsy, but it's a difficult part of the body to access, you have to somehow get in there without touching the heart or lungs. It requires a highly specialized form of radiology. He was trying to see if they could fit me in today, but you need a bed in case something goes wrong. So he was waiting to see if they had a bed. If not today then tomorrow. He hoped to call back soon.

When he hung up, Michael said, "Let's just go in."

"He said he'd call back."

"You want to sit around here all day, waiting for a call?"

So we drove back to the hospital. I remember thinking, as I showered and dressed, you're about to become one of the pushed-around. It's stupid, but I was glad to take my car. Michael's was still parked at Betty's house. At least I could drive myself in. After three thousand miles it looked a little the worse for wear; desert dust had covered most of the paneling. And Michael had to clear out the passenger seat before getting in. There were soda bottles and potato chip bags and empty boxes of Entenmann's. He didn't say anything, he just threw it all on the backseat floor.

At the hospital, they sent us to the cancer center. I don't know the names of the wards, Michael had taken control. I was the kid at his elbow on the first day of school. He spoke to the people at reception, he gave them my name, he mentioned Dr. Liebman. But they seemed to know who I was, I was in the system. They gave us a room to wait in, and a nurse came around to take my blood pressure and pulse. Michael had brought his computer with him; he did some work. I had taken a book along from his apartment, a three-in-one volume of Raymond Chandler, and tried to read. *The Big Sleep* was the first novel. "It was about eleven o'clock in the morning, mid-October, with the sun not shining and a look of hard wet rain in the clearness of the foothills."

But it was hard to get pleasure from the fact that the story was set in LA while I was stuck in a room without windows. It even had a curtain across the front you could draw for privacy.

Around eleven, I saw one of the doctors, Dr. Farnham. For some reason, she had on a black cocktail dress with her mask. But she was a very careful and self-controlled person, she had a comforting presence. The impression she gave was, whatever you've got, it's something we've seen before. It's something we've thought about.

She asked me to take off my shirt and examined me again. She said, it's rare to see such classic symptoms for an SVCO. Liebman had used the same phrase. It meant an obstruction to the superior vena cava, the main vein that flows into the heart. In my case, it was almost completely constricted. This is why you have all these veins popping up. The body is a wonderful machine. If the highway is blocked, it uses the side streets.

Michael asked, "Is there any news on the biopsy?"

"I'm optimistic."

After she left, I said to him, "I'm sorry you have to sit here all day. You must have things to do."

"Nothing that matters," he said.

Later Dr. Farnham came back with a couple of residents. She said, "I hope you don't mind, I thought it might be useful for them to look at you, for diagnostic purposes." They were both young women. So I took my shirt off again, one of them felt my pulse. The tumor can sometimes cause a slight delay between the heartbeat in one wrist and the other.

Michael gave me a look when they were gone.

"What?" I said.

"This is just an excuse for you to get undressed in front of women."

But it cheered me up.

I wasn't supposed to eat anything, but Michael went out to get some lunch. He came back with a chicken sandwich. "I hope you don't mind," he said. The smell of it drifted toward me. "I've spoken to Mom. I spoke to Miri too. They're both planning to fly out. Mom said she'll be here tomorrow, Miri is coming on Thursday, which means she only has to skip one class. What are you thinking."

"Nothing."

"What?"

"Thank you for calling them," I said.

"I think that you should probably talk to Mom yourself."

It was almost five when they sent me in for the biopsy. My son and I had been sitting there for seven hours. But it was nice to sit with him. I asked him what he was working on. He told me, but most of the time we didn't speak. His phone rang and I heard his side of a conversation with Betty. He said, I don't know when, we just don't know. Yes, I know, he said. Me too.

Something had come to an end, that much was clear. Whatever I was doing was over. But I didn't know what would replace it, if anything.

At one point Michael asked me, "Do you think you knew you were sick, when you drove out here? On some level . . . I mean, is that why you came?"

"I thought you didn't believe in that kind of thing."

"I'm a little more open to it than I used to be. That's something Betty taught me."

He liked to say her name in front of me.

The radiologist looked like Alberto Tomba, the Olympic skier. I don't know why this occurred to me. Tomba la Bomba was his nickname. He had a broad face and a thick chin and broad shoulders. I imagined him going snowboarding on the weekends, he seemed more like a heart surgeon than a radiologist, someone who lives by his nerves. A dude. Michael asked him, how many of these biopsies have you done? And he said, not that many. Nineteen or twenty. It's a very specialized procedure, you don't get a lot of opportunity. But he didn't seem particularly concerned.

Michael, of course, stayed in the waiting room.

There were several nurses working with the doctor. I lay down on another narrow bed—I had to take off my gown. They covered my legs with a blanket. He applied a cold gel to my chest and pushed the scanner around in it. For some reason, everything seemed to be happening very quickly; he took an ultrasound, and looked at it, then he ran back to take another. From time to time he made a mark on my chest. Then they all stepped out of the room, and the bed slid into the long tube. I held my breath, and slid out again. He worked with a pen in his teeth and held something in his hand that crackled like a transparency sheet. But these are all vague impressions. Mostly I just lay there with my eyes closed. Suddenly I felt a prick against my skin and then a deep incision. But it was over as soon as I felt it. The whole process was repeated several times.

Afterward, they wouldn't let me walk. I said, "This is ridiculous, I'm perfectly capable of walking on my own. If you're worried, I can lean on my son, but I feel fine." It didn't matter, I had to wait for a nurse to come with a wheelchair. Then she pushed me to another part of the hospital.

My room had one of those beds you can bend into almost any shape. It had a window, too, which overlooked another part of the building. I became aware of the time of day: sunset. You could see its color reflected in some of the windows.

Before she left, the nurse took my blood.

Dr. Liebman stopped by to introduce himself. "I come bearing pills," he said. He had a beard, which meant his mask sat awkwardly on his face. It was a dose of steroids, a hundred milligrams of prednisone. He said they're so effective you can't give them ahead of the biopsy because they affect the results. But you might have a little trouble sleeping, it's usually better to take them earlier in the day.

"When can I go home?" I asked. The pills were small but chalky and hard to swallow.

"We need to take a chest X-ray in a couple of hours, to make sure your lungs are okay. But if that looks good you can go."

"Can I eat something?"

"Sure. But don't go to the cafeteria. At least, that's my advice."

He had a good bedside manner. He talked to you as if he was a little embarrassed to be meeting you in these circumstances, because if it were up to him he'd rather invite you for a beer. But these things weren't up to him.

"What should we eat?" Michael asked, after he left.

"What do you want?"

"I noticed Socalo as we drove in, which has a good reputation. I think there's also a Thai place. I'm sure we can order something on DoorDash, but I don't know how they'll find us here."

"A green curry sounds good."

"It may take me a while."

"That's fine. You could use a break. You're a good kid."

Even the way I talked to him made me feel older.

While he was gone, I called Amy but forgot about the time difference. The phone rang several times, I was about to hang up. "Hello," she said. "Hello?"

"It's Tom."

"Hey, Tom." You could hear that she was lying down; she spoke very close to the receiver. You could almost feel the heat of her breath.

"I'm sorry, did I wake you up?"

"No, I'm awake. I'm awake now. Has something happened? Are you all right?"

"You talked to Michael, right?"

"Yes, Michael called. I'm sorry, Tom. I'm so sorry."

"Well, what can you do."

We spoke for about half an hour. She asked me about Michael. I told her I met his girlfriend, well, I don't know if she's his girlfriend. But they're clearly very close.

"What do you mean, you don't know."

"I haven't seen them kiss or hold hands. But they seem to expect to see each other or at least communicate every day. He called her at two in the morning." I described his apartment to her. I said, "He's been wonderful. I wouldn't be here right now if it weren't for him."

"Is there any news? What did the doctors say?"

So I tried to tell her. They measure their words carefully, they don't make promises. It depends on what I have. But they say most lymphomas respond well to treatment. Some of them are curable.

"They said that?"

"I think that's the word he used. But they don't like to tell you until they know."

We also lay in silence for long periods; it was nice to have her on the other end of the line. I said, "There seem to me three basic possible outcomes." When I talk like this, I hear my father's voice. He was always preparing himself against reality by arranging it into useful bullet points. But what can you do; at a certain point, this is who you are. "The first is, I'll have a hard six months, and after that my life will more or less go back to normal. Whatever that means. The second is, this will be a hard six months, and after that I'll have to live with it for many years, and deal with it from time to time, and see what happens. The third is, I'll be dead soon."

"You sound very calm about it."

"I'm just trying to think it through."

"I'm sorry, I didn't mean any criticism."

"No, I know."

"Is Michael with you?"

"He's getting me something to eat. I wouldn't talk like this in front of him."

She said, "I've been very angry with you."

"I'm sorry. I shouldn't have left like that, without telling you."

There was another long silence.

"For years I was angry, because I knew you were going to leave me and I was scared. I think that explains a lot of my behavior. Aren't you going to say anything?"

"I'm thinking about what you said."

"You're a very frustrating person to live with. I don't want you to die before we make up."

"No."

"I'm scared, Tom. I shouldn't say this to you, but I'm very scared."

"That's all right. I don't think it's really sunk in for me yet anyway."

But we talked about other things, too. I told her about Brian, I told her about seeing Eric. She had signed up for a course at the Art Students League. She was going to do classical drawing but figured she could do that at home, so she signed up for a sculpture class instead. They were working with clay; for that you need a kiln.

Eventually Michael came back with the food.

"What time's your flight?" I asked, holding up a hand.

"The taxi's coming at seven; we land around lunchtime. I need to get some sleep."

"Okay. Good night," I said, and she said, "See you tomorrow."

We actually had a very pleasant meal. He brought spring rolls too, and two kinds of rice; the curry was still fairly hot.

I hadn't realized how hungry I was. There was a TV in the room, and we watched the Dodgers playing the Giants as we ate. It made a useful background noise.

"What are you thinking about," he said, during a commercial break.

"You're all being very nice to me."

"Well, you've got cancer."

"That's what I was thinking. It seems a lot easier to be nice to me when I'm like this."

"That may be true," he said.

Around nine o'clock the nurse came to take me for my X-ray. She brought another wheelchair. It was all a charade. I stood up first to use the bathroom on my own, then sat in the chair. She wheeled me to another part of the building, we had to take an elevator. Michael walked behind us, she kept bumping into things. The wheelchair had sticky steering. The hospital at this time of the night had grown very quiet; the windows were dark, the corridors echoed. The X-ray department seemed completely deserted, but then there was a light at the end of the hall, and a woman was waiting for me.

What happened next I can't completely account for. Maybe it was because I hadn't eaten all day, and then I took a lot of steroids, and then I had a lot of calorie-rich food. I had to stand up for the X-ray and press my chest against a vertical scanner, while the technician retreated to another part of the room. I also had to hold my hands above my head. She wanted me to do this twice, she needed two scans.

After the first one, I told her, "I have to sit down for a minute." There was a gurney in a corner of the room, and I sat on that. My head had started to fill with blood, at least that's what it felt like, and I was aware that my body had entered system protocols my conscious mind could no longer intervene in.

She said, "Take as long as you need."

Then I stood up for the second X-ray. I wanted to get this over with and go home. Afterward, I thought, just make it to the wheelchair.

By the time I opened my eyes again, I felt better. My head was clear, but there were several other people in the room; some of them had wheeled in a piece of heavy medical equipment. There was also a pool of liquid on the floor. I thought they must have spilled something, but then I felt the wetness between the legs of my gown.

I said, "Where's Michael?"

He was almost in tears, he looked pretty freaked out. He wanted to hold my hand. For the first time since I came to Los Angeles, he looked like a kid.

After that, nobody let me walk anywhere, and I didn't try to. Michael told me later he thought I was dying. My eyes rolled, until you could see the whites, and my body began to spasm. His first thought was, there's nobody around, he had to get me to another part of the hospital. So he grabbed the wheelchair and started pulling me away; he had to wrestle the technician, who was pulling back. It would have been funny, he said, if you had seen us. I guess you had to be there, he said. He didn't know she'd already pressed the crash button; the doctors were on their way.

They wheeled me back into my room and helped me into bed. Then they left us. I said to Michael, "I don't think I'm going jogging tomorrow."

"No."

"You must be wiped out too."

"I don't want to leave you like this."

"Well, it's not the Comfort Inn. But I'm fine. The doctors said I'm fine. I'm in good hands."

My car keys were in my pants, which he'd been carrying around with him in a plastic bag. I took them out and gave them to Michael so he could drive home. After that I was alone.

Even at night the building seemed to emit a faint hum, like an old refrigerator. For a while I tried to read. Then I turned off the light and shut my eyes; then I got bored of that and played with my phone for a while; then I listened to some music. The steroids made my face feel tight, I don't know if that was psychosomatic. It was like the current of electricity running through me had been slightly increased; not uncomfortably so, but enough to make me aware of it. I wasn't supposed to stand up so they gave me cardboard bottles to piss in. The nurse was meant to collect them but they built up on my bedside table over the course of the night, like a cardboard skyline.

If you can't sleep, you just lie there thinking. Michael used to be a terrible sleeper. I'd stop by his room before going to bed and find him staring at me in the dark. He lay awake worrying about school, he was one of those kids who basically didn't want to be with other kids. He was waiting for adulthood. There were mornings we could barely persuade him to get dressed. At night when he lay there I tried to talk to him about it. I asked him, on a scale of one to ten, how was your day. Three, he might say. Is that okay, is that acceptable? What do you mean acceptable, it's over now. But is three good enough. Good enough for what? To make you go back tomorrow. I guess, he said. In that case, it's acceptable, right?

We had versions of this conversation many times. For years, when I went to bed with Amy, this was the kind of thing we told each other, even at the worst.

Something else I remembered. Five or six months after we started going out, Ethan Konchar got in touch with her. He was in Boston for a conference. He wanted to buy her a drink. She didn't know whether to mention it to me, but then she mentioned it. There was a dinner, which he had to go to; she was meeting him beforehand at the Harvard Club. He's taking you to the Harvard Club? Like, this is the kind of guy . . . but still I had to watch her getting dressed and putting on makeup. When she came home a few hours later, I tried to make a joke of it, which only pissed her off. Finally she admitted, he asked her to go away with him. He was flying to London in a couple of days and offered to pay for her ticket. Amy felt terrible about it, her guilt reactions were always off the charts. Maybe she even started crying. What are you crying about, I said, did you want to go away with him? No, but she'd wanted him to ask. Of course you did, I said, which was what I felt. But it was also the right thing to say, it made the moment easier.

Every few hours one of the nurses came to check on me. I'd watch her in the light from the opened door, pulling some kind of machinery behind her. Slowly disentangling the wires. Once she said, "Oh, goodness." She didn't realize I was awake. She took my blood pressure, she took my temperature, she measured my pulse. But she always forgot to take the bottles away.

You forget how long the night is. The part that counts is ten o'clock until five in the morning. That's like a whole day at school or the drive from Westchester to Pittsburgh. On a scale of one to ten, how was your day? Michael was talking to me, I was the kid in bed. Maybe I did sleep a little in the end. Then the window curtains started graying, someone was doing the rounds with coffee and tea.

Amy came at lunchtime; Michael was with her. He'd brought sandwiches from Bread Head, which he said he was pretty excited about. She wore jeans and flats and a soft gray jacket, her travel uniform. To get to the airport she'd had to leave the house at sunrise, and still had that look you get from flying, where you put up a front all day, and the front gets a bit dented. Even at her age, she has to deal with male attention and doesn't want it but can't help trying to be nice about it. I don't know why I thought that. Maybe because seeing her again after a week you see her the way she actually looks, like, if you ran into her in the airport lounge you'd think, I hope I sit next to her. I'm not making much sense. I mean, it's strange to see her like that, without all the other layers.

It was probably easier with Michael there. He called Miri, too, on FaceTime and propped the phone up on my bedside table. (After disposing of my piss pots himself.) So we all had lunch together, though it was almost four o'clock in Pittsburgh, and Miri had nothing to eat in her room but a box of graham crackers.

"How's it going over there," I said. Her image was a little stop/start, the connection wasn't great.

"It's going."

"That doesn't sound good."

"It's fine, I'm fine, it's just . . . a lot all at once. I'm having a good time." But then she went off camera for a while, I don't know what she was doing. "I'm just very worried about you," she said.

"Don't worry about me, you've got enough going on right now."

"What does that even mean."

We also got in a stupid argument—not me, but everyone else. Michael asked me if I'd seen the doctor yet, and Amy said, let's just . . . let's not do this now. Do what, what do you think we're doing? She meant, in front of Miri; at least, that's the interpretation that Miri reacted to. Like she was just the kid and had to be sheltered from the conversation at the grown-up table. I don't know. I also got the feeling that Miri and Amy had been talking a lot on the phone and Amy knew things about Miri's state of mind that people weren't telling me, but maybe this was just paranoia.

I said, "They took my bloods again this morning. If those are fine, they said I can go home."

"Just like that?" Michael said

"Well, I've got another scan at two. But after that I can go."

"I'm not sure I can drive you," Michael said. "I've got a class."

"Of course, you do what you need to do."

"I don't want to leave you. I'm also supposed to do a shift tonight at the restaurant, but I can probably get out of that."

"It's fine, your mother's here."

"I just feel bad," Miri said. "I feel far away."

"You're exactly where you're supposed to be," I said.

If you eat in bed, you get a lot of crumbs on you, and since I was only wearing one of those thin blue gowns, after a while you feel like, this is squalor. On top of everything else. I also hadn't taken a shit all day. In the morning I tried but the nurse had to wheel me to the bathroom, and then she was waiting outside, and I sat on the pot, feeling the pressure. There's only so long you can make someone wait, but when I got up, she had gone, and I had to walk back to the bed myself, pushing the wheelchair, which was fine, but also made me think, what's the point. But all of this was contributing to my state of mind.

Then the doctor came, and I said goodbye to Miri. It was Liebman. One of the nurses had brought another wheelchair. "I can walk," I said, "it's fine."

Michael said, "You can sit in the wheelchair." But he had to go—he was supposed to TA, and it was a half-hour drive to campus, including the walk from the parking lot. "I think I gave you the keys?" he asked his mother. "I mean, at the apartment." They had stopped off on the way to the hospital, to leave her suitcase, and so she could freshen up.

Amy found them in her purse.

"I can push him," she said, after he left. "I've always wanted to push him around."

I don't know who that was for, me or the doctor. She had obviously made a decision about how to behave and was trying to stick to it. And the decision was, treat him like a typical guy, who can't be trusted to look after himself. Later it occurred to me, this is just the new reality. She's acting like this because you're sick. If you're sick and might die, this is how people treat you, especially if they love you. You should just enjoy it.

They took us to another part of the hospital, we had to go up an elevator. Then they led me into another small room. The nurse said, "Do you plan to sit with him? This'll take about an hour."

"I don't have anything else to do."

"Is there any chance you might be pregnant?"

"No," she said.

But they made her sign a waiver. Apparently, the procedure

234

involved infusing me with a dose of radioactive glucose; for an hour, I just had to sit there, while it went through my system. Being in the room with me involved some slight exposure. And afterward, I mean after the scan, I was supposed to avoid the company of children and pregnant women for another six hours. I said to Amy, "You don't have to do this," but she only touched her fingers to my lips.

The nurse put a cannula in my left forearm; it took her a while to find a vein. And even when she found it, the blood wouldn't flow. She had to try several times.

Amy said, "I'm going to look away, if that's all right." But we got there in the end.

"How's Miri?" I said, when we were alone.

"She's great, she's fine . . . I'm not sure her roommate is the person I would have chosen for her. But I guess that's why you go to college, to learn how to deal with people."

"What's wrong with her?"

"She has a boyfriend, so already twice this week, Miri had to find somewhere else to sleep."

When I started getting angry, she said, "This is why I didn't want to tell you."

I was lying down, or half sitting up, on one of those narrow hospital beds; Amy sat in a chair. It was hard to keep the gown over my knees. She tried to make a joke about it, maybe to change the topic. It was a strange situation. But you could only keep up this kind of tone for so long. At one point I said, "Amy, I just wanted to say . . ." and she said, "We don't have to talk about it."

I looked at her and she went on, "You can talk too much about everything, I don't know if it helps. I remember this when my dad died. Some things just happen. It's not like if you don't talk about it, you don't know what's going on. You know. I'm sorry, I just mean, it's okay. I don't blame you for anything. I don't even blame myself. Does that make sense?"

"Yes," I said. But we had to sit there for almost an hour; of course we talked.

Then the nurse came and led me away. She suggested I use the bathroom first; they had a special radioactive toilet, with a warning sign on the door. Afterward, I lay down on another long retractable bed, which slid into the mouth of the machine. I was supposed to keep very still, otherwise it ruins the image. As I lay there I began a conversation with my mother on the phone, I was trying to work out how to tell her. Hey, Mom. Listen, I've had some bad news. I tried to compose a few emails, too. To my brother and Brian Palmetto and Sam Tierney. I imagined writing one to Jill. Hey, look, I just thought I'd let you know ... it turns out ... but I didn't know how to begin. It felt strange not to acknowledge something about what happened the last time I saw her, but that also seemed totally unimportant now. And Amy was waiting outside.

It took about fifteen minutes. Then a voice came through the machine that I was finished, and the retractable bed started to retract. The radiologist walked into the room; she had long dark-brown hair tied in a ponytail. Sometimes you try to imagine what these people are like outside their official capacity, but that's partly because you start to see yourself as they see you, as this very limited person.

"I'm sorry," I said. "I'm not very good at getting up."

"Take as long as you want."

But I made it to the door, and then Amy was there with the wheelchair.

We didn't really know what to do next. It took us a while to find the room where I spent the night. Amy pushed me. The hospital floors are very smooth, and for some reason I said, "Is it fun," and she said, "What?"

"I mean, like when you're a kid, and you go shopping."

We got there in the end; I recognized one of the nurses. But I had to wait for a doctor to discharge me, and they had other things to do. So we sat there, waiting. It was almost six o'clock, I was starting to get hungry again. I was on a lot of steroids and one of the side effects is increase of appetite. My face felt tight, a little swollen. I was also sick of the hospital gown; the bed still had sandwich crumbs in the sheets. Michael had brought me a change of clothes from his apartment. I could feel Amy watching me as I dressed, the bruises under my heart, the veins on my stomach.

"Get a good look?"

"I'd kiss you," she said. "But you're radioactive."

Eventually Dr. Liebman came. He knocked first, and we said, come in. I don't know why this seemed strange to me, I felt like I should offer him a drink. My bloods were fine, he said, I could leave, but first he wanted to make sure I could get around without the wheelchair. So the three of us made a little promenade along the corridor, with Amy on one side and the doctor behind me, in case I collapsed.

"Look at him go," I said, in my best Chris Berman voice. But the truth is I felt a little shaky. Anyway, I passed the test. They weren't giving out grades, it was just pass/fail.

"When do we hear from you?" I asked.

"We have our clinical meetings on Friday morning, and by that point, the biopsy should be in, we'll have the scan results. We'll call you around lunchtime."

He wanted to say something else but didn't know what.

"Don't think about that now," Amy said. "We have three more days where we don't have to think about it."

Then it was just the two of us again. Amy carried my bag, I held her hand. Getting out of a hospital is like escaping a casino, they don't make it easy for you. We passed the wall with art from the children's ward, we stood in the elevator with an old man lying on a gurney, tubes coming out of his nose, being pushed around by a nurse wearing a pair of Kobe Mambas. We walked through the lobby, past the potted ferns, the reception desk, with wandering steps and slow (for some reason that phrase came into my head) and then out of the glass doors onto Wilshire Boulevard, in the level early evening sun, with palm trees lining the road. After two days in the hospital the outside world looked . . . the planet seemed very bright and loud, cars buildings people.

"What do you want to do now?" Amy said.

"What do you mean?"

"We're in LA. The kids are all grown up. Michael said he won't get home till after midnight."

"Let's go home," I said.